Running From My Shadow

Danielle Nicole Bienvenu

ALSO BY DANIELLE NICOLE BIENVENU

Against All Odds: The Ruby Princess

Le Beau Coeur-The Beautiful Heart

My Brother's Keeper

He's Mental, That's Why!

The Gilded Mirror

Changing Stripes

The Elopement

Escaping Lila

Roberts, Dana, 21.

Once In A Lifetime

Taming of the Free Spirit

The Right Kind of Perfect

The Life of Virginia Wargenheimer

Sarah's Secret

RUNNING FROM MY SHADOW

Copyright © 2013 Danielle Nicole Bienvenu

All rights reserved.

ISBN-10: 1482086654
ISBN-13: 978-1482086652

Originally published in e-reader format Smashwords July 2011

DEDICATION

Inspired by someone I once loved more than life itself.

Dedicated to my Grandma, Annette Hammaker Valentine. I love you and your firecracker spirit.

Dedicated also to the man who was captivated by her until his death, a grandfather I never knew, Thomas Howard. Rest in Jesus's arms.

RUNNING FROM MY SHADOW

CONTENTS

Acknowledgments	i
Chapter One	1
Chapter Two	7
Chapter Three	11
Chapter Four	15
Chapter Five	20
Chapter Six	26
Chapter Seven	38
Chapter Eight	43
Chapter Nine	59
Chapter Ten	65
Chapter Eleven	69
Chapter Twelve	78
Chapter Thirteen	94
Chapter Fourteen	97
Chapter Fifteen	100
Chapter Sixteen	107

Chapter Seventeen	111
Chapter Eighteen	120
Chapter Nineteen	123
Chapter Twenty	132
Chapter Twenty-One	137
Chapter Twenty-Two	147
Chapter Twenty-Three	159
Chapter Twenty-Four	164
Chapter Twenty-Five	167
Chapter Twenty-Six	172
Epilogue	180
About the Author	183

DANIELLE NICOLE BIENVENU

THE COAT OF ARMS OF DANIELLE BIENVENU MAY NOT BE
REPRODUCED WITHOUT PERMISSION. MAY BE PUNISHABLE BY FINE
OR WHEN IN EUROPE, IMPRISONMENT. REGISTERED WITH THE
EUROPEAN ARMORIAL.

CHAPTER ONE

It is amazing how the entirety of my life has been spent running. My existence has been composed of fears, and more often than not, from people I have never met or from the ones I let go. For example, my grandfather Flannigan died from a stroke in his fishing boat. He was fifty-two years old, and single with a beer in his hand when his number was called. He was with his friends enjoying the beauty of nature like he normally did, or so I've been told, and wham in one second everything he knew came to an end. But in truth, everything he knew ended many years before that. My grandmother was eighteen when she met my grandfather. I know nothing of their romance, mainly because my grandmother hates him so much she refuses to talk about it. They married. She was nineteen and he was quite her senior when his first child, my father, was born. A few years later my aunt was born. Grandmother said Grandfather grew jealous and paranoid, checking her mileage on her car when she returned from work, fearful that she had been sneaking behind his back with some man. Of course, it is easy for my Grandmother to make Grandfather look like the villain when he is not alive to defend himself. Finally, Grandmother grew tired of his mess and divorced him. She remarried shortly thereafter and he followed her steps and married someone else. The woman my grandfather married eventually turned up on my grandmother's doorstep and told her that she couldn't stay with my grandfather anymore. She told Grandmother that Grandfather was still in love with her and she could not compete with her. My grandmother dismissed her. My grandfather did in fact become divorced, again. When he died on his fishing boat he had a picture of him, my grandmother, my father, and my aunt tucked inside his wallet, pressed to his chest. The first time I heard that story I had decided for myself that I would never live without the one person I truly loved and all at the same time I felt a strange pull of understanding that someday if I weren't careful that would be me. I am twenty-four years old, which to most would not even amount to a drop in a bucket worth of years. But it is only now that I recognize what has been my main driving force: the fear of myself. I remain assured that everyone who has ever breathed a breath of life has had their own set of doubts and fears and a low self-esteem is often listed among them. I on the other hand, am not writing about a case of low self-esteem. I am writing about self-realization and the fear that undoubtedly accompanies it. I am married, a college graduate, and yet I am still like a child running from his shadow. Better yet, a child running with his shoes untied while running from his shadow. I hear nothing but the pounding of my shoes on the pavement and the firm beating of my own blood pulsating to my heart.

    I feel a steady vibration in my pants pocket. I slow my running down to a pace and two seconds later, to a halt. I reach for the cell phone in my pants pocket and rest my hands on my knees. My back hunches over as I try to steady my breathing long enough to answer a phone call. Sweat pours from my brow and my cool skin tingles now that I have stopped running. A dryness has formed in my throat and the top of my tongue has stuck to my pallet. I swallow hard, allowing the last trace of saliva in my mouth to travel down my throat. My nostrils burn as I breathe out. I flick open the cell phone and bite my lip, wondering if I should really take this call. After a brief moment's pause, I decide to press send to accept it. She would have found me anyway.

"Collin? Where in God's name are you?"
I surveyed the wilderness beyond the road I was standing on, "It doesn't matter."
"Of course it matters. Where are you?" I could hear the irritation in Karen's voice. I had told her years ago that I didn't want any children and now here she was, possibly pregnant. I could envision her outraged with anger and scared as hell that I was out running while she was sitting on the toilet lid bouncing her leg uncontrollably. I knew she was wearing those raggedy pink slippers that used to be fluffy but had once left their pieces of fuzz along our kitchen rug. I would get it good when I returned home. I couldn't say I would blame her if she chose to throw a slipper at me.
I breathed a heavy sigh and looked toward the horizon. In the distance I could see faint clouds

rolling in. I knew they would eventually overtake the wilderness with darkness and threaten the road with rain. I also knew I should go and be with Karen. It was the choice any sensible person would choose. So I went. "I'll be there in ten minutes."

"Alright, hurry up. I have been staring at the EPT stick for the past twenty minutes waiting for you to show. I haven't flipped it over yet. I thought you were just going out for milk." So did I, I thought. And yet I ended up here. I'd been here so many times before.

On the drive home I could do nothing but think of what had led me to this point in life. I had met Karen fresh out of college, when working with a lumber company near Sea Breeze. The money was decent and I was happy enough working with my hands on the open land. It wasn't what I went to college for, but I had decided the last month of college that I didn't want to become a lawyer. I wasn't at ease in any courtroom I'd had the chance to intern at. My spirit longed for nature and it was Julia who had encouraged me to pursue what I loved. I'll get to her in a minute.

I met Karen my third month at the lumber yard. She was bright and definitely not the sort of woman I expected to see as the new secretary. She had no desire to wear mud boots, even when the coastal rain floods washed in she would often tramp through the lumber yard to find our boss in her heels. In Sea Breeze no woman wore heels, except this one. Karen, had a fiery spirit about her. It was she who first suggested we go on a date, regardless of the employee dating restrictions at the company. I'd been surprised by her boldness and said yes. She went so far as to suggest we go out for sushi and I will admit, I found it refreshing to take her up on the offer. I liked not having to pick the place or make the decision on how to ask her out. I picked her up the night she asked me out. After many dates, it only seemed normal to go forward in the relationship. After all, we seemed to like each other enough and she knew nothing about my past, which was a definite perk for me.

Three years later I asked her to marry me. She insisted that I leave the lumber yard, because as she said, I could never have a real career in that. I wanted to make her happy by putting my law degree to use. I had initially applied to Harvard during my senior year of high school, but now I realize that was only to appease my worrisome nature. I didn't want to end up like my parents: community college, unaccomplished, drowning in normalcy. I was accepted in to Harvard Law only to have to turn it down for the lack of funds. But now I wonder if my turning it down was out of fear of paying loan payments for the rest of my life, even if I did own my own practice in the future. Anyway, Karen encouraged me to rekindle the law fire and so I did. I ended up staying in Sea Breeze with a job at a local practice pushing paper work. Sometimes I still question if I had known I would be shoving paper work inside an office if I would have gone to college at all. My dad used to be a lawyer. He was sensible, bored, and safe. He and Mom had three kids, which could have even been named Sensible, Boring and Safe.

I would Safe considering I am the youngest of my siblings.

And now I have come to terms with the fact that I might always be Safe, just like my father. I know it sounds obtuse to view it that way, seeing as how my wife might be carrying our baby. I love Karen, I do, and one of the last things I would want is to hurt her. But I have. And she doesn't even know it.

I pull into the driveway and make my way to our bathroom door. I catch my wits and knock on the door. Karen doesn't answer. I push the door open and see her sitting on the toilet lid, her face in her hands.

"Karen?" I call to her.

She lifts her head and her brown hair falls around her neck. She has watery eyes. "We're not pregnant. Just like you wanted." The air rushes out of me but still I can't help but feel relieved and guilty at the same time. I feel responsible somehow for this. I open my mouth to speak but cannot find the words. Karen shakes her head and pushes past me to exit the bathroom.

CHAPTER TWO

I met Julia my junior year at college. She was gentle, very much so and her eyes always remained unguarded. I admired that about her, especially since I could not help but guard myself. She was also unpredictable. It goes without saying that I admired that about her as well. We went to the same community college, which was how we met. She was studying in the education building which was the closest to the law building on campus. I bumped into her one Fall afternoon. I remember the heat outside was starting to cool off and a breeze was just starting to make its home in the season. Instead of yelping when I bumped into her, she laughed. She had one of those contagious laughs, you understand. The kind of laugh that even if you are having the worst day, which I was when I met her, you end up laughing yourself. And I did. It was because I was having a bad day that I didn't notice her, but looking back I cannot see how I didn't notice her to begin with. I was sick with the flu and said so. I blurted it out right after I apologized. I was in a hurry to get home for the simple fact that I felt miserable, well, that and once I had bumped into Julia I was embarrassed.

She smiled up at me with her big violet eyes and said, "It's okay," And it was, "I'm Julia."

"Collin." I said.

She offered to help me feel better. Her offer certainly took me off guard. She said while interning at elementary schools she had encountered too may flues to not know how to treat them. I was unsure at first, mainly because I didn't know her and I didn't want her coming down with the flu herself, but she insisted and soon, it felt like I had known Julia my entire life.

We walked to the Drug store across the street and Julia piled my shopping cart full of juices, Vitamin C, four packages of cough drops, and a value pack of Kleenex.

When I opened my mouth to protest that I could take care of myself and didn't need all those items, she threw a package of herbal tea in the cart and smiled at me rather smugly, "Before you tell me how you don't need these things, think of how you will feel at 2 a.m. Besides, you owe me. You did run into me." There would be no arguing with Julia. I could recognize that then as I do now. As soon as we stepped out of the store I said, "Crap. I forgot to buy some Prego soup."

"Prego?" Julia wrinkled her forehead like she'd just witnessed a mutant cross the street, "You need chicken noodle. It's the best." I thought about protesting but she added as she slipped her shades on, "I have some at my place."

"How do you know I'm not some ax-murderer?" I asked her.

She gave one of her contagious laughs again but this time it made me want to shrink, "Because," she said, "ax-murders don't wear purple penguin socks." I raised my pants legs to survey my socks, surprised and at the same time mortified that she had noticed. My grandmother had given them to me for Christmas last year and as much as I hated to sight of them, I didn't have any more clean socks left to wear. I tried my best not to look at her but could not help but wonder what sort of student would be in her classroom, because at the time I thought she was studying to become a teacher.

We walked in silence for a few minutes until eventually I had to ask, "So why do you want to be a teacher?"

"I don't," she stated matter-of-factly, "I want to be a school nurse."

"Which would explain why you want to doctor me up." As it turned out, her place was just around the block and though I refused to acknowledge it, the woman intrigued me. She wore a plaid scarf, a black tank top, shorts, and flip flops. But then again, I wore purple penguin socks so who was I to judge.

Here she smiled and grabbed my wrist, pulling me with her toward a dorm complex in front of us, "Exactly," she said. Julia fished her key out of her pocket and turned it in the lock. The door made a buzzing noise and let us in.

"But why do you want to work at a school?" I knew I was being nosey, but I didn't care. Everything about this girl was odd to me, like a new species.

She shrugged, "Because I can't have kids."

I wanted to slap myself. I stood in place as she kept walking and had to jolt myself to follow her toward her dorm room. "I really am sorry, I shouldn't have asked."

"No, it's no problem. It's just I can't have kids. Life is life you know." Julia unlocked her dorm room door and twisted the knob. She entered her dorm and threw her scarf on the counter, "The way I see it, if I can't have kids then I might as well be around a lot of them. Maybe then it will be like I will have my own one day," She turned back to look at me, "The answer to your next question, though you have yet to ask it, is why I want to be a nurse. I want to help people; it's as simple as that." Julia shoved me on her sofa, "Just you sit there while I make you some chicken noodle."

"Why not a doctor? You could be a pediatrician," I asked her.

"Because," she called from the tiny kitchen adjacent from me, "my dad is a doctor. That would be too easy." I understood perfectly.

CHAPTER THREE

"So what are you studying?" Julia asked as she entered the small living room which was really more like the size of a box. She held a bowl of chicken noodle soup in her right hand with the spoon already stuck in the bowl and in her left hand she held a glass of water. "Sorry I don't have anything else to offer to drink," she said.
I shrugged it off and thanked her for the drink and the soup. Julia took a seat opposite of me in a small rather uncomfortable looking recliner.
"Law" I said as I took a sip of the soup. It was certainly hot. I pulled back and made a noise through my teeth.
"Don't burn your tongue," she said.
"Too late."
Julia crossed her legs and leaned her elbow on her knee, "Why law?"
I shrugged again, this time realizing I was prone to shrugging when unsure of what to say. I cleared my throat, "It just seemed like the most logical choice."
"Ah."
I blew on the soup and attempted another sip, "Ah?"
"You're playing it safe."
"Excuse me?" For someone I just met today she was certainly being forward with her opinion. And, as much as I hated to admit it, really good at reading people. She was right on track.
Julia waved her hand and elaborated, "Let me

guess, your dad is a lawyer."
"Hit the nail right on the head." I sneezed really loudly and snot began to pour from my nose. Julia ran to give me a tissue and I blew my nose on it.
"Wow," I said, "that was really embarrassing."
Julia smiled while suppressing a laugh, "Think nothing of it. But what about you? What do you like to do?" Truth be told I hadn't thought about it much. "Come on, there must be something," she prodded.
I thought for a moment then said, "The lumber yard."
"What?"
"I like working at the lumber yard in the summer."
"Well then why aren't you doing that?" To me the answer seemed obvious.
"Because the object of working is to earn enough money to well... live."
Julia looked toward the tiny window on the far side of her living room and nodded. "I know how you feel. I'm sorry I brought it up. All I am saying is life is short. You should do what makes you happy and be with who makes you happy." Julia waved her hand and turned to face me again.
The urge to ask her the next question overtook me, "Who makes you happy?"
"You mean..." Julia's violet eyes met mine.
"Yeah, do you have a boyfriend?"
She wrinkled her nose as if she'd just seen another alien, "No," she said, "not by far but my mom makes me happy."

"Oh?" I wasn't expecting that answer. A girl who loved her mother and didn't have a boyfriend was a rare combination these days.

Julia went on, "I guess you could say we have our own language," Julia saw that I was confused as to what she meant so she continued; "She's Deaf" she clarified. I nodded. I didn't know what to say. She noticed me struggling for words so she filled in the gap. "She was born Deaf. She met my father in school. I never thought my mother was different from any other mother until kids told me. You know how cruel children can be." Here I nodded again. "What about you? Are you close to your parents?" I let out a whistle and leaned back on her sofa, "No. My mom died when I was ten and my father, well; he was more of a worker than a father. I'm not saying that to be harsh, he just was. Some men are good at their job, other men are good fathers. I think he just didn't know how to react to Mom's death... how to cope." I remember feeling a lump in my chest. Julia scooted toward the edge of her seat waiting for me to say more. I liked that she didn't ask me questions then. "I have two older brothers. I was the youngest at ten so I think my dad thought since we were older we could handle it better. He wanted everyone to think he was okay but he wasn't." Seeing that I would say no more on the subject, Julia retrieved the plastic bag from the drug store and took the cough drops out. She offered me one.

"I'm sorry about your mother," She was genuine, I

knew that much.

"Thanks," I said. I popped the cough drop in my mouth as she took the soup bowl from my lap and placed it in the sink. When she returned I asked her, "I don't even know your last name."

She smiled as if to say I was charming in my ease of getting to know her, "What has that got to do with anything?"

I fought the urge to shrug again, "I suppose it doesn't."

"Douglas."

"Flannigan," I said and couldn't help but smile at her. "See, all this time and you didn't even know my last name. I could have been a killer."

"Yes, but you are forgetting, killers don't wear purple penguin socks."

"Of course not."

Julia walked toward me and took a seat by me. She leaned back on the sofa and crossed her legs. I took note of her long blonde hair and the way it fell into a mess, like she hadn't a care in the world. I told her thank you for the soup and she handed me a Vitamin C tablet. She held out my glass of water, "I told you, I will make you better yet," she said.

Minutes turned into hours and time ran all too quickly that afternoon. I knew it was late, I knew I should be going, but I couldn't bring myself to leave. Talking to Julia was like talking to an old friend that I hadn't seen in ages. I began to wonder where she had been all my life.

CHAPTER FOUR

I edged toward Karen, waiting to see what I should do next. There was no manual for this sort of thing. Every man knew talking to a woman was like walking a tight rope over flames. One mistake could bring you to your end. The beauty of being married to Karen, or so I thought when I married her, was I wouldn't have to talk much. But now here I stood in front of her and she was waiting for me to say something. Somehow I managed the words, "I'm sorry" but soon after I said them I wondered if I said them out of guilt or sincere regret. I never imagined this scenario. In college I never thought I would have kids to deal with because I didn't want to be my dad, but not only that, I knew Julia wasn't able to have children and in the past I never pictured a life without her in it.

Karen turned around to face me. I could see tears starting to burn hot on her face. She looked me up and down, noting my sneakers.

"What happened to going out for milk?"

"It was a nice day," I quipped.

"It was a nice day," She repeated. "Why is it that running is more important to you than whether or not we have a baby on the way, Collin?" I knew not to say anything else right now. She was venting and if I interrupted that would only make the situation worse. Karen continued, "I knew we didn't plan on having children, but when I realized I might be pregnant I grew excited. A baby... A part of you and me..." She wiped her cheek with the back of her hand, "I had hoped you would learn to be excited about it just as I was but now I see that was too much to hope for." I took a step toward her and grabbed her hand. "Why are you so afraid of this?"

"I can't do it, Karen. I just can't." My words took me by surprise.

"Why not?" Karen peered into my eyes then her own eyes flashed and she jerked her hand away from me, "Let her go. She's not here, I am. I am the one making my life with you. Why can't you embrace that?" Karen's shoulders shook and I knew sobs would come soon.

I reached to take hold of her shoulders and wrap her in my arms but instead she grabbed her purse off our bed and trekked out of the house. There would be no easy way to resolve this one.

Thirty minutes later the phone rang. I was coming down with a headache; probably more form worry than anything else. I didn't know where Karen was but I did know she didn't want me to find her. I leapt for the receiver and pressed it to my ear. The phone didn't even get past the first ring by the time I answered it. I never would have guessed who was on the phone.

"Collin," A deep voice said, "it's me. Listen um... Karen's here." My father. It was my father. I hadn't spoken to him in months, not since his birthday in January. It was April now. Despite myself, I couldn't help but wonder why Karen would see him of all people. "I just thought you would want to know."

I stood in the hallway with the receiver pressed to my ear for a few seconds before I replied. "When did she get there?"

"About twenty minutes ago. She's not so good." I nodded. I knew this was my dad's way of saying I had screwed things up big this time. "I think you should give it an hour and come pick her up. She is in no condition to drive home."

"Okay," I said, "Keep her safe."

I found myself sitting on the sofa in our living room staring at our wedding picture. Karen had been all smiles then. I knew we didn't have the dream life but I thought we were happy. We'd been married for three years and now I found myself questioning what I could do to make her happy again. I checked the clock every five minutes and when an hour had finally passed I got in my car and drove to my father's house in The Ridge subdivision. The red lights seemed to take forever. I parked in the driveway and surveyed Karen's car before I went in. Did she have her things packed in the back seat? Was she planning on leaving me?

Instead of knocking on the door I walked right into Dad's home. When I did, Karen craned her neck around to look at me. She was sitting on Dad's blue and white sofa with a tissue in her hand. Dad sat opposite her but he rose once he saw me. He came over to shake my hand. I pumped his and nodded. This was as familiar as we got. I thought he would offer for me to sit down but instead he walked me to the kitchen and confided in me. He answered one of the questions I'd had since he first called me.

"Listen Collin, Karen has been coming here every Sunday since my birthday. She says she wants us to be a closer family," Dad cleared his throat as though he suddenly found it difficult to talk, "She told me that she wants a family of her own," He paused to look at his shoes then back up at me, "Now I'm not saying you should do that, but I think it would help ease her concerns."

"Concerns? What concerns?"

Dad leaned in closer, fearful that Karen might hear him. "She thinks… well, she thinks that you don't love her."

"Love her? Of course I love her!" I was outraged. I knew my voice rose on the last sentence but it did not matter in that instance. I surmised that Karen could probably hear me from where she sat in the living room.

"A woman is a funny thing…"

"You're telling me!"

"Just hear her out, Collin," Dad pressed his lips together like what was coming next was truly hard for him, "She thinks she is your second best and that she will never measure up to…" Here Dad motioned his head to the side as if to imply some forbidden name, "Now I know, I know how difficult it can be to let someone go. But you have Karen now. You have to think of her." I nodded, wondering where in the hell he came up with this considering he had seemed to wallow in his own grief after mother died without being a father to us kids. I knew to keep my mouth shut. As much as I refused to admit it to anyone, I still loved Julia and always would. I knew that. But I also loved my wife and the past could not be undone. I think that is what unnerved me the most.

"Right." I stalked out of the kitchen.

When I reached Karen in the living room I stood there and heaved a sigh. Karen peered up at me, her brown eyes puffy. She rolled the tissue over in her hands. I squatted down next to her and took her hand. "I love you, don't you know that?" Karen's lip quivered. "I'm sorry. I'm so sorry I hurt you." I took her in my arms. She pulled away and smiled at me. That was my hint that everything was going to be okay. "Come on," I said rising to my feet, "let's go home."

CHAPTER FIVE

"Where are you taking me?" I shouted to Julia.

"Oh, nowhere in particular." She was having fun with this, I knew. She'd already put a blind fold on me and now we were cruising around in her jeep. She had to be driving at least one hundred miles per hour. The woman was a speed demon. She sighed over the radio. "Okay, okay, if you must know…" She waited for me to nod enthusiastically, "I'm taking you to meet my mom." Just then I felt the jeep hit a bump and I gripped my seat with my right hand. Julia leaned over and removed the blind fold. I blinked at her. "Welcome home."

Her grin, much like her laugh, was contagious. I found myself rushing to open her car door and when I did she took my hand in hers. "She's going to love you. Don't worry."

"Easy for you to say."

We walked up the steps and Julia walked right in. It was odd to see her not ring the doorbell or knock first, but after being around Julia for a while I began to understand why and soon adopted the action as my own. Her mother couldn't hear her knock anyway. Julia walked cautiously through the house, to make sure her mother was fully dressed because as Julia later explained to me, she sometimes liked to walk around in her robe. The house smelled like black cherries, I remember that much. I looked at a candle burning on the coffee table and whipped my head around to feel Julia tugging on me.

Her mother was a beautiful woman, and now I knew where Julia got it from. She had a big smile, much like Julia's. Julia brought her thumb to her chin then down to the middle of her chest. Her hand was open much like showing the number five sideways. Mom, she said. Julia ran up to her mother and embraced her warmly. She signed the same motion again. She then brought her two index fingers together then turned and smiled at me. I found myself watching her fingers move rapidly to spell my name C-O-L-L-I-N. I was expecting a hand shake or a simple nod from her mother, if anything, but instead she greeted me with a hug. She pulled back and smiled. She repeated some of the same motions Julia had just used. C-O-L-L-I-N so nice to meet you. As she did so, her mouth moved a bit more than Julia's had as if she might be sounding out the words, but I knew she wasn't.

After Julia's mother, whose name I learned was Alice, offered me something to drink, the three of us retreated to the living room. Once we sat down, it appeared that Alice had suddenly forgotten something. She signed something to Julia and left the room.

"She said to stay here," Julia said then she leaned toward my ear and whispered, "I think she likes you."

A minute or two later Alice returned to the

room with a plate of cookies and her husband in tow. Snicker Doodles, she signed to Julia and Julia translated it for me. "They're made from scratch," Julia added. I could already feel my mouth beginning to water. Alice signed to me, though I wondered why because she knew I didn't understand her language. But as she began to sign I realized I was already starting to pick up a few American Sign Language signs. Then there was one at the end I did not recognize but I knew it meant husband. Julia later confirmed my guess. C-O-L-L-I-N, meet my husband, Frank. When Alice signed Frank she made the world renowned symbol for "okay" then touched it to the tip of her nose and threw it down, much like she was sneezing. My eyebrows jumped, unsure what to make of the sign for her husband's name. Julia tapped me on the arm without signing, "My dad sneezes a lot."

Julia's father stretched his arm forward and pumped my hand, "You'll have to excuse her," he said smiling, "My wife has a sense of humor."

Despite myself, I began laughing. Alice brought the Snicker Doodles toward Julia and I. We each took one and relished it. I looked to Frank, pondering what I could say and noticed that he was covered in dirt. Julia looked to me then to Alice. She signed while she spoke, "He has been battling the chain saw all day so he can cut trees in the back." I nodded, knowing the difficulty of such a feat. Julia explained while speaking and signing at the same time that I worked at a lumber yard during the summer and that I liked it very much.

I watched her in awe. I marveled at the way she moved her hands so smoothly and the ease with which she translated. Julia, I had already learned, made everyone feel at ease. She truly was a marvelous woman, a wild unattainable creature that I began to fear I loved. Everything in me was telling me to run as far away from there as I could because I'd grown too attached and yet I couldn't bring myself to leave. Julia turned toward me and winked. She grabbed another Snicker doodle off the plate and handed it to me. Yes, she was perfect in my sight.

When it came time to leave, Alice sent me home with the left over Snicker Doodles. Frank had wanted to know my secrets for easy tree cutting so I had disclosed them. Julia embraced both of her parents, not caring whether she was covered in dirt from her father or not. Julia and I stood outside of the door and a wave of courage washed over me. I lifted my hands and though they felt awkward I signed Nice to meet you. Alice's smile grew and her eyes widened. She turned to her husband and tugged on his sleeve. Frank smiled back at her and waited for her to sign something to him. Alice signed rapidly and Julia began to laugh.

"What's that mean?" I asked. Julia shook her head. "No, come on, tell me. What did she say?"

"She said," Julia told me as we walked on the

driveway to her jeep, "that she likes you very much and can see why I love you."

It had only been two months since I first met Julia but already every time I saw her there was a pounding in my chest and if anything the pounding of my heart increased even more so when she told me that.

My mouth grew dry and I still don't know how I had the courage to ask her, "Do you love me?"

Everything stood still. There was no past or future, only the present. And there was no one else except the two of us: my beautiful Julia and me. I began to feel sick. Butterflies danced in my stomach as I waited for her response. My breath became shallow.

Julia toyed with the keys in the ignition and finally met my gaze. I can still remember of vulnerability on her face when her eyes met mine and she smiled half-heartedly from nervousness. It was the first time I'd ever seen her nervous. I can recall the way the coolness of fall felt on my skin as it blew in to the jeep, the exact way her hair was styled, everything about that moment. When she breathed the next words, I thought my heart would burst. "Very much."

I reached my hand out to cradle her face and stroked her cheek with my finger. I knew this much: there had never been a happier man in the entire world. I pulled Julia toward me and engulfed her in a kiss. "Good," I said as I pulled back, "because I love you too. Very much." As she smiled, I noticed a stray tear falling from the corner of her left eye. She pulled at my shirt and I held her even tighter. It was then I knew I never wanted to leave her.

CHAPTER SIX

Even days after our profession of love, as I pressed forward running all I could focus on was Julia. She ran alongside me as the Texas sun rose from behind an entire field full of pine trees. Years later I would run this path, thinking of her and the only thing I could be sure of: the love we felt for each other.

I knew the heat would soon be pounding its fists on my skin causing me to thirst. I wasn't much of a runner before Julia, I'll tell you that right now. Once she got me started running, I ran to clear my head. After her I ran nonstop. My family, though small and formal were worried sick that I would run myself to death. But you see, I was convinced that if I ran hard enough and fast enough she would come back. But of course, looking back I had no knowledge that heaven would crash to the ground. All I knew was how at peace I felt.

"Do you ever think about God?" Julia breathed as she turned the corner and whipped her blonde ponytail around to look at me. Beads of sweat were forming on her hairline framing her face and I could see pools forming above her lips and across her forehead. Her skin was flushed from the heat. I could see the splotches running had made on her porcelain skin and wondered why I had never met her until now.

"Um," I glanced down at my worn sneakers then

back at her, "sometimes."
"What do you think?" That was Julia, bringing random topics to the surface and hurling them at you when you least expected it.
"I think... Well, to be honest I don't know what to think." I paused for a moment to gather my thoughts some more. We had discussed the topic of God before and we both believed there was one. We had already talked about the planets colliding and matter forming out of nowhere and everything that entailed, but we had yet to discuss a personal God. I knew this was the topic she was aiming for. I shook my head and Julia tugged at my shirt as she continued to run. This was my cue to continue. "I think that maybe he or she could be watching us like some science experiment to see who goes wrong, who does right, and who was a waste of time and energy."
"Really," She said.
"How often do you think about it?" I faltered.
"Most of the time," I scrunched my eyebrows. Julia saw my confusion so she began her thoughts on the subject. "Oh, I went to Sunday school when I was little, every Sunday and holiday. I know what the Bible says but only recently as in say the past year have I begun to truly think about it," She waved her hand as she continued to run. I watched her take in a deep breath. "There has to be more to this life than what we actually see."
"Or what?" I challenged her. We often debated.
"Or else everything would be in vain. Take for instance the sun rising over there," Julia pointed to

the giant orange ball of a sun rising in wilderness, "Why would it be there if someone, God, didn't want us to enjoy it? I refuse to believe that this all happened by some chance, a mere coincidence. It's like saying you and I stumbled upon each other by chance."

"Didn't we?"

"No," Julia shook her head at me. I found myself captivated by her eyes until she turned her head forward again. "I think everything has a purpose. And if there is a purpose there has to be a personal God. I've been reading what the Bible says and actually trying to take it in this time."

"And you think that's the answer?"

She paused a moment and pursed her lips in thought. I could tell she was weighing her words. "I do."

"I wish I could be as easily convinced as you are. Your certainty is intimidating." It was then that I first realized I'd never been certain of anything in my life, except that I loved Julia.

"There is no point in being certain unless we're certain about the right thing. I've been listening to the pastor at Mom and Dad's church. I went at first because they had a lady that signed for Mom. I thought it was great that they would include her like that instead of making her feel like an outsider," I nodded because I knew how important her mother was to her. I remembered her mentioning visiting the church with her parents, "But now I don't know. I think there is more to it than just simply living life as it comes."

She licked her lips, "The pastor spoke last time about salvation. I think I'm going to do it next time."

"Do what?" I asked. I sincerely had no clue what in the world she was talking about.

"You know, give my life to Christ." Here Julia slowed her running to a stop and leaned on her knees. Birds, undoubtedly Blue Jays and Cardinals, were chirping from their perches in the pine trees.

"You honestly think God himself came down to save us from our own plight? Why would he do that?"

She straightened up and panted, "Because he loves us. He created us, Collin. He wants us to live life how it was meant to be. This doesn't have to be it for us. We can have so much more in this life and the next."

I squinted my eyes then, partly from the sun and partly from trying to understand exactly what she was saying. It was all new to me, but I had to admit that the notion of there being more to this life tugged at me. Deep down in my inner most parts I had always hoped there was something more than devastation, wars, broken homes and stolen dreams. "Would you come with me?" She asked me. "Please? Look, I know you aren't sure about this whole thing and that is okay. I want you to come with me for it. It's important to me that you be there." She took my hand and before I realized it the next words that formed on my lips were "Yes."

I still recall the first Sunday morning I went to church with Julia. Her parents were excited to see me in the pew beside them. I'd gotten better at deciphering the signs exchanged between Julia and her mother so I didn't need Julia as my translator all the time. I tugged at my dress shirt. The collar was pinching me. I knew it was because I hadn't dressed like this since my aunt died and that was years ago. Julia beamed at me once she saw me and planted a kiss on my cheek. She squeezed my hand as the pastor called her down to the front. I had been thinking the entire sermon about just what exactly the man was saying. Strangely enough, it made sense. But I wasn't ready to make the sort of commitment Julia was so I remained in the pew. I watched the pastor baptize her after he announced she had been saved. Her parents took pictures and people clapped wildly.

Once the service was over, Julia immerged from a side door in the front. Her hair was still wet from the baptismal but she was beaming with an excitement I'd never seen before, not even from Julia. I still found the whole baptizing thing rather strange. I handed her a spare towel her parents had asked me to hand to her. They were off talking with the pastor.

"How do you feel?" I asked her.
"It's the best feeling in the world." I marveled at her words. "Well, that and loving you." She

smiled at me with that contagious grin of hers.
"I've been thinking," I said, "that maybe next time I'll do it too."
"Do what?" Her eyes brightened, "Accept Christ?"
I nodded, "Mhmm."

The next Sunday I went with Julia and her parents as promised. Between the Sunday Julia was baptized and I accepted Christ, Julia had volunteered to go with me to meet the pastor so I wouldn't be uncomfortable asking questions to a total stranger. She had even sat down to talk with me throughout the week about making my decision. My mom was interested in the notion of a loving God but that was before she died and ever since then the term "God" was absent from our vocabulary at home. In the end, I decided to invite my dad and brothers to witness the event but none of them showed. I had hopes that they would be there but even as I invited them, I knew they wouldn't show. I tried not to be disappointed but evidently my disappointment showed through enough for Julia to notice and give me an extra squeeze of the hand. She always did that… squeezed my hand when I needed support.

I remember fidgeting with my slacks as the pastor called me up. I held true to my decision and the pastor prayed with me. I repeated his words and accepted Christ into my life that day. I heard nothing but those words and their weight as I stood in the midst of the congregation. The idea that someone would die to save me from my sins, much less God himself, seemed radical to me. As a matter of fact, it floored me. All I knew was I had spent my life without God in it and I had a lot of time to make up for.

There was a potluck after my baptism. Complete strangers I didn't even know rushed to me with congratulations and gave me hugs. Hugs were not a commodity in my home, at least not after my mother died. As it was, I was only accustomed to hugging Julia. Julia made me close my eyes at the potluck. When she told me to open them, there was a book wrapped in starred wrapping paper in my hands.

Julia's smile slid to the corner of her mouth, "I know you said you didn't have one so I thought…"

I ripped the paper open in a flash. In my hands was my own Bible. My first Bible. My mother had one and read it daily not long before her death but after she died, I never saw it again. I knew my father had gotten rid of it. But now, standing there with Julia and the Bible in my hands I could do nothing but think of my mother. A lump formed in my throat. My heart was so full I wasn't sure could feel anymore love. Scratch that. I hadn't known such love from another person ever. It was as if Julia had brought my mother to me on the most important day of my life. "Thank you," I said as I engulfed her in a hug and kissed the top of her head, "You have no idea how much this means to me."

Julia and her parents had been there to

support me in the biggest decision of my life. Alice had signed Proud to me, the same sign I'd seen her give Julia before. I secretly wished I could have the sort of family she did. After the potluck, we went our separate ways. It was the last I heard of them until Julia called me later that night.

I was lying down to go to sleep when my cell phone rang. I immediately knew it was Julia and answered it right away. I smiled, thinking of her.

"Collin!" She wasted no time in saying, "It's my mom. She's in the hospital."

"How? Why?" I was stunned. I'd just seen her hours ago and she was fine.

"She cut her hand making dinner. She cut it wide open. She was bleeding so badly that dad had to get me to drive to the hospital while he tried to stop the bleeding."

"Is she going to be okay?"

"Yeah, I think so," Julia exhaled into the phone, "they are stitching her up now. I'm so angry I can't see straight."

"Why?" I asked simply.

"It's the nurses. Please, could you---"

"No need to say it. I'm on my way." I slammed down the phone quickly. Even as Julia had begun to ask me to leave for the hospital I was already zipping my jeans and walking out the door.

When I arrived at the hospital, Julia was pacing in the lobby. I grabbed her by the shoulders and pulled her into my arms.

"It's the doctors too," She picked up where our phone conversation had left off. I waited for her to explain everything in her own time. The smell of antiseptic consumed my nostrils. I hated that smell. "They look at her like she is some freak!" Julia had buried her head in my chest but now lifted it so that I could see her face. Tears were starting to form in her eyes. "Dad and I were trying to explain to them that Mom is deaf and we could translate for her. But no, they wanted Mom to tell them directly what happened to her. They won't let me translate. It's like they think Dad or I did this to her. None of their staff interprets and it's hard for Mom to sign with just one hand to people that don't understand her. They look at her like she is some sort of animal!" I'd seen Julia angry before but nothing like this. "She's not an animal! She's a human being!" Julia pounded her fists on my chest and sobbed, "She's my mother! I don't understand how they could treat her this way at a hospital." If it were anyone else I would have pushed them away when they pounded on my chest and told them to gather their senses. But this wasn't anyone else. This was Julia. "There aren't any interpreters near here. They won't let us call in distant ones," Julia looked at me, hopeful, "Collin please, do you think you could pretend you don't know us and interpret for her?"

"Interpret?" I was flabbergasted. "Julia, I don't know enough…"

"But you know more than anyone else around

here. The interpreter from church is in Ohio for two weeks. There is no one else. And you've spent time with her, you know her."

I said nothing. Instead, I grabbed her by the hand and walked to the nearest elevator.

Julia pushed the button and we rode two floors on the elevator before we stepped off. She turned left and led me through a long hallway filled with nurses and people coughing in the hallway. We walked through glass doors and entered the Emergency Unit. When we arrived there a nurse was on her hands and knees by Alice's cot scrubbing blood from the floor. My stomach turned in knots. I knew she'd lost a lot of blood and I knew this was hard for her. I'd grown close to Julia's family. I could only hope I could pull this off.

"Who are you?" A nurse questioned me. I hadn't been prepared for that question.

"I'm uh…" I stumbled.

"He's an interpreter," Julia interrupted, "He's here to interpret for my mom." She looked to Frank and Alice.

Frank nodded at me. Behind Alice's eyes there was a quiet desperation. She looked exhausted.

"Well," the nurse grumbled like it was the biggest inconvenience she'd had since the dinosaurs roamed, "I guess so." She retrieved Alice's chart off the door and positioned her hand to take notes.

Alice raised her left hand. I steadied myself.

Cut hand. Make food. Scream. Frank get towels. Julia drive here. I knew Alice used broken sentences and easy words for my benefit so that I could understand her. I wouldn't use the broken sentences to translate to the nurse. They needed to know Alice was intelligent. And she was. Julia often told me she thought her mother the smartest person she knew.

I spoke up. "She says she was making dinner and cut her hand. She screamed and her husband, Frank, retrieved towels and tried to stop the bleeding. She says her daughter drove her to the hospital."

"What was she cutting?" The nurse raised her brow in question. I knew she was doing this to see if I really was an interpreter or not. I blinked and she repeated her question.

I looked to Alice and signed What food you cut? I wasn't sure I had even signed that correctly. I was better at comprehending American Sign Language than actually signing it. I could feel the nurse's eyes burning into my skin.

Cucumber, Alice signed.

I lifted my hands then realized I had no idea what she signed. I grew more nervous.

Cucumber. Alice noticed that I did not know that sign, which was obviously why she had left it out to begin with. Her fingers shook as she tried to make it simple for me and signed the individual letters. C-u-c-u-m-b-e-r.

"Cucumber," I blurted out once I knew what Alice said, "She was cutting a cucumber."

The nurse brought her chart of notes to the doctor and twenty minutes later they released Alice. Alice's hand was still incredibly sore from the stitches but she extended her arms and wrapped me in a hug. Thank you, she signed. Thank you so much, Collin. I smiled at seeing her sign for my name. Alice and Frank had adopted it for me. It was a C above the brow to signify my worry. I shrugged and nodded. Julia wrapped her arm around me as we exited the hospital's lobby doors. I felt more comfortable with the Douglasses than I did with my own family. I'd wanted a family like that when I was ten years old and my mom died. But now that I had a new family and salvation I still wanted something more.

I figured if God could save me from my sins, he could certainly help me with something else. I wanted to take Julia as my wife.

CHAPTER SEVEN

Once Karen and I got home I took a can of Ravioli out from under the cabinet and placed it on the counter. I retrieved the handheld can opener and secured it to the top of the can. I was twisting the knob on the can opener when Karen walked into the kitchen. I waited for her to say something. She said nothing so I continued to open the can of Ravioli. I knew she was watching me. I took the lid off the can and poured the Ravioli into a pot. I opened the refrigerator and grabbed a head of lettuce and began pulling it apart to make a salad to go with the Ravioli.

Once I set it down on the counter I realized I needed carrots, onions, salad dressing and croutons so I went back to the refrigerator to grab those. I already had our bowls sitting on the counter and dropped the ingredients for the salad into each bowl. This was about as fancy as my cooking got.

Karen folded her arms and looked down at her feet, "Thanks for making dinner."
"You're welcome." I slid the knife into the carrot. She was about to say something else, I was sure of it.
"I saw you."
"Excuse me?" I threw the slivers of onions into the bowls and walked over to the stove to stir the Ravioli. I hadn't the slightest idea what she was

talking about, especially since she hadn't said one word since we left Dad's.

Karen leaned in toward me, "I saw you with Julia at the hospital." I winced when Karen said Julia's name. I knew something ugly was about to head. I fought to keep my voice steady. "But how?" I clanked the spoon on the inside of the pot and sat the spoon on the spoon rest. There was no way Karen had been there that night. She was talking crazy and I wondered why she chose now after she waited three years to tell me this.

"I had just moved to Sea Breeze that summer to be with my sister. She was having her baby at the hospital. I stepped outside of the room to take a breather. It had been a long labor for her and I was going to get some ice chips on the fourth floor." The fourth floor. I hadn't been on the fourth floor the night Alice cut her hand open. I was on the fourth floor the night Julia was in a coma. I closed my eyes to brace myself for what Karen would say next. "I saw you sitting outside Julia's room. You were on the floor with your head in your hands. You lifted your head and looked ahead. I thought you saw me. I wondered what I should say but you looked right past me like you didn't see me. You walked back inside her room and I peeked in. I know I shouldn't have but I did. I saw you kiss her hand."

I backed away from the stove and grabbed the salad bowls to place them on the table.

Excruciating memories were starting to come back to me and I had Karen to thank for it. I didn't want the reminder. "Just stop it, Karen."

"You looked so in love and heart broken. I didn't recognize you when I first saw you again at the lumber yard but then later I knew it was you." She walked over to me and placed her hand on mine. "Sometimes I feel like even now, even now that we are married you don't see me. It's like you're still in love with her. I can't compete with a dead woman, Collin…"

"I told you to stop it," I warned her. I squared my jaw and could feel my fists clenching. My throat was going dry and my heart had fallen.

"I'm your wife…"

"Enough Karen! Enough!" My shouting took me aback as much as it did Karen. I'd never shouted at her before. However, it wasn't enough to detour her.

Karen heaved a sigh. "I know that you were hurting, that you are still hurting and I'm sorry, I am. But I am your wife, Collin, not Julia."

I threw the forks on the table. I could smell the Ravioli burning in the pot but suddenly I didn't care anymore. "She was! Julia was my wife, Karen! You expect me to just forget everything? I lived before you, you know…" I brought my fist to my mouth to stop myself from saying anything I'd regret.

"You don't want a baby, Collin because it wouldn't be Julia's baby. You don't want me…" It was as if a lump formed in Karen's throat because her voice cracked, "You want her. It's like I've already lost you and I can't get you back. But

guess what Collin? You're about to lose me too."
Karen held her gaze into my eyes for a few seconds.
I gritted my teeth, "Don't you ever mention her name again, do you understand me?"
Tears brimmed Karen's eyes as she walked past me to head up the stairs, "I understand you perfectly."

I knew Karen like the back of my hand. She was going to get a shower. I had twenty minutes before she would immerge for dinner. Twenty minutes before I had to compose myself again and pretend that everything was okay. I placed my hands on the tile counter top, shifted my weight onto it and dropped my head. Things were irrevocably screwed. It didn't take a genius to figure that out.

I love Karen for her. It wasn't like I had this misconceived notion that she was the reincarnation of Julia or anything. Karen had been so understanding when I finally told her about Julia. She'd never said a word about seeing me the night Julia was in a coma at the hospital and that thought enraged me. It was as if I had been living the past three years of my life with a liar under the same roof. It wasn't as if I were a horrible person. Sure, I misunderstood her desires at times and sure, I wasn't the best husband, but I was trying to be who she needed me to be. It was like I was hobbling around with one leg instead of two and everyone treated me the exact same as when I had both legs. People pretended like I was not maimed because it suited them. I had a huge weight on my shoulders that never left. It stayed there not matter what I did.

I swallowed, remembering the time I went to church and saw Julia give her life to Christ. I had no idea he would take her so soon. I hadn't been to church since before Julia died. It wasn't that I was angry with God; it was that it hurt too much to go. Every service would remind me of her and I knew it. The summer we met, we'd read the entire Bible together. It seemed like we had a billion questions that could not be answered quickly enough. Now it seemed like there was only one question left: How could I ever find any rest? It was because of her that I came to Christ in the first place. I shook my head and brought my hands to my face. I hadn't been giving my burdens to Christ. I hadn't been doing what the scriptures said to do: Come unto me all who are weary and I will give you rest. Matthew 11:28. My eyes began to sting. Tears were threatening to fall. I'd spent four years running from the truth.

CHAPTER EIGHT

After Julia died I lived in denial. I didn't think she was really dead. Before the doctor pulled the cord he suggested I see a grief counselor. Dad of all people suggested I go as well so I did. I still see the counselor from time to time when I feel like I need to. Of course, Karen knows nothing about this. If she did, my head would have fallen long ago. I told the counselor that I felt like Julia was still alive. I insisted that I could feel her lying next to me when I was asleep and when I woke up in the morning it was like I could still smell her perfume lingering in the air. It was like she was standing next to me when I did the dishes in the kitchen and I could have sworn I heard her voice when I'd take the dog out for a walk. The counselor said it was called shock and though it seemed difficult at the time, I would eventually grow out of it. But I haven't. I don't mention this to anyone because I know they will only worry about me. I've never been one to have people fuss over me. Even now, after four years, it is like Julia, my Julia, is still next to me. It's like her presence is still here and she never died to begin with. I have to remind myself that she's gone and she's never coming back. When I feel Julia beside me I tend to run to clear my head. Though I try, I can't let her go. I don't know how to.

I suppose I should tell you what happened to take Julia from my world. We had been married only three months before she died. I had to pick up some milk from the store after work. Julia had called at lunch and asked if I could pick up some milk so that she could make a casserole for dinner that night. I'd said sure but was in a real rush to get back to cutting some lumber at the lumber yard since my break was already up. I completely forgot about it when I drove home after work. Julia was already home and preparing dinner when she saw I didn't have a carton of milk in my hand. She didn't nag me, she never did. Instead, she heaved a sigh and said not to worry about it. She told me to go get a shower and she'd be back in a few minutes with the milk to finish dinner. She'd gotten off earlier than me like she always did being a school nurse. She still had her uniform on and she looked exceptionally sexy. I couldn't wait to undress her piece by piece and run my hands over her soft, delicate body. The thought made me tingle inside.

I wrapped her in my arms and told her I was sorry and I would make it up to her by lighting some candles over dinner. She'd smiled at me like she was looking forward to it. I gave her a kiss and released her from my arms. Julia picked up her purse from the floor and rubbed her temple with her right hand. I could tell she had a headache and now it made sense why she called me to get the milk. She didn't say bye when she left. She just grabbed her purse, looked over her shoulder and smiled at me. I swallow at the memory of it all and a lump forms in my throat. It seems like yesterday and yet as if I've lived without her for a hundred years.

I'd unbuttoned my flannel shirt then and kicked off my shoes. I walked toward the bathroom and ran the hot water in the tub and pulled the shower lever. I undressed and threw my wallet and cell phone on the bed. I recall being tired that day, just mentally and physically exhausted so I ran my hands through my hair and stepped in the shower. The steam felt so good on my tense shoulders. My mind ran as I wondered how else to make dinner special for Julia. I planned to lay out some Aspirin for her headache and make her favorite drink, Mango Tea. I knew exactly where the candles and the lighter were for a romantic ambience. I thought I heard a noise as I washed off the soap from my body, but decided I hadn't. No one would be calling because they had no reason to. Julia was at the convenience store getting milk and would be home soon. My family wasn't exceptionally personal and my co-workers and boss knew not to call me after hours unless it was an emergency. After all, it was a lumber company not the American Government.

I finished washing off and turned off the water. I pulled the towel from the hook on the wall and began drying off. It was then that I heard the phone ring. There was no denying it this time. I squinted my eyes, surprised that anyone would be calling. Maybe Julia forgot an ingredient or needed to know if I needed anything else while she was there. I knew it was farfetched but I supposed it was a possibility. I quickly wrapped my towel around my waist and ran to the phone in our bedroom. It always smelt like lavender in there. Julia kept the entire house smelling nice. Water droplets were falling off my body as I picked up the phone.

"Hello," I said in a rush.
"Mr. Flannigan?"
"Yes?" The voice on the other end was definitely not my Julia's. In fact, it wasn't anyone I knew. It sounded like an older lady bearing bad news. And that is exactly what it was: the worst news of my life.

"Mr. Flannigan, it's your wife, Julia. I'm sorry Sir, but there's been an unfortunate accident. We need you up at St. Joseph's Hospital. She's in room number 401."

The air rushed out of my body. I wanted to know what happened but it never occurred to me to ask. I just wanted to get there as quickly as possible. I didn't finish drying off. Instead, I threw on an old t-shirt lying on the floor and my work pants covered in lumber chips that I wore earlier and ran out the door.

I bet I was driving 120 miles per hour on the way there. It seemed like the lights took forever and more than once I honked the horn at the cars in front of me. I turned on my emergency lights and finally people got the idea that I was in a hurry. I swerved into the parking lot and jerked the keys out of the ignition. I ran full force through the lobby doors and up the stairs. I didn't have time to wait for an elevator. The pungent smell of antiseptic invaded my nostrils and I found myself wanting to puke. Surely God wouldn't take her from me now. We'd only begun our life together.

I raced to the fourth floor of the hospital and bolted to room number 401. Nurses scolded me as I ran but I didn't care. My Julia was there and she needed me. By the time I sprinted to her room, her parents were already there. Alice's eyes filled with tears as she turned to look at me. Frank backed away from the bed. Alice released Julia's hand, the same hand Julia's wedding band was on. With her parents moving I could see Julia lying nearly lifeless on the hospital bed. Her blonde hair spilled over a pillow propped behind her neck. Tubes were shoved up her nostrils and a giant tube protruded from her mouth. A loud machine pumped oxygen into her body. I watched the air rise and fall within her. Wires were wrapped around her head connected to a machine that showed strange lines and beeped every now and again. I felt like I had fallen through the floor. I tried to pace myself as I walked toward her. I knew my breathing was loud as Frank and Alice watched me. I could hear Alice sob as I took Julia's hand. I stretched out my right hand to stroke Julia's cheek.

"Julia," I said aching with the sound of her name, "I'm here Baby. Don't worry; we're going to get out of here." I kissed her cheek.

Frank opened his mouth to say something but before he could the doctor walked in to find me standing next to Julia.

"Mr. Flannigan."

"Collin," I corrected him.

He nodded, "Collin, I hate to be the one to tell you this but your wife was shot at the convenience store." My eyes searched for a wound on Julia's body and I immediately saw dried blood on the other side of her head. My fingers ran over the wound and I felt like I had suddenly taken a heavy blow. I knew she wouldn't be getting out of here easy. "A couple of kids robbed the store. Your wife must have been in line to purchase something when they arrived. I only know what the police informed me of but," here he paused, "they said eyewitnesses saw her try to calm down the boys. They must have not liked that and shot her in the head. Your wife is one brave woman," the doctor sighed, "I'm sorry Collin but your wife's case is difficult. The bullet went straight to her brain. The bullet has placed her in a coma and even if we wait years from now the chances aren't good that she will come out of it."

I couldn't believe words actually spilled from my mouth, "What are her chances?"

"About one in five thousand," I fell back and rested on a corner of Julia's hospital bed. "I'm really sorry, Collin. I know this can't be easy on you. If you need anything I'll be back in the morning. Until then nurses will check on her around the clock and they'll page me if anything happens," he paused again and said, "You should probably prepare yourself for the worst. With this sort of injury it becomes imperative to consider all your options."

Frank spoke next, "Options?"

"Yes, whether or not to pull the plug," With that the doctor left the room. Frank, though hit with the impact of the doctor's news, was forced to translate to his wife. Alice sobbed again.

I kneeled on my knees and laid my head on Julia's hands, "Come on, Julia," I breathed, "don't leave me now. Not now." I kissed her hand and closed my eyes.

I prayed hard that night. Alice and Frank left about an hour later to leave me and Julia alone. Frank offered something to eat or drink from the cafeteria. I shook my head and said nothing more. I spent majority of the night coiled next to Julia's bedside. I woke up somewhere around four a.m. and decided I needed to get out of there for a moment so I walked just outside the door, looking for a nurse to check on Julia again. They were all busy at their stations so I slid to the floor and sat there. I buried my face in my hands and wondered when Julia would wake up. I lifted my head a few minutes later and felt tears finally begin to swell in my eyes. I walked back to Julia and picked up her hand. I studied her wedding band. Her hands were so small and fragile compared to mine. They were a lot cleaner too. She wore pink nail polish which was quite fitting given pink was her favorite color. I took her hand and squeezed it tight.

Someone must have notified my Dad of Julia's accident because the next morning Dad tapped me on the shoulder. I slowly lifted my head from Julia's bed. I'd been seated next to her and leaned on the bed by her hands, holding them. I was incredibly groggy and the tears from earlier made it difficult to see straight. "Son," was all Dad said and handed me a tiny carton of orange juice much like the kind I used to drink in the elementary school cafeteria. He held a breakfast burrito in his other hand. I shook my head. Dad stood there a while without saying anything else. He placed the juice and breakfast burrito on Julia's bedside table in case I changed my mind. For once in my life I was actually thankful that he didn't try to get personal with me. As I sat in the plastic chair by Julia's bed I began to wonder for the first time what Dad must have actually gone through when he lost Mom. I won't say I felt sorry for him but I began to understand him and why he acted the way he did a little better.

I was surprised that he stopped by Julia's room, especially considering he never knew Julia well because he didn't know me very well. Julia used to wonder if maybe he didn't like her since she had been the one to urge me to pursue what I liked for a living, working at the lumber yard, instead of following the boring bill of my father in the realm of law. I knew he wasn't pleased about my career choice but as he stood there I knew he no longer blamed Julia for my decision, if that is he ever did. He left about thirty minutes later.

Life went on like this for about six months. I would wake at 4 a.m. and go running to clear my head. I'd return to the house, take a shower, feed the dog, dress, and fix myself some breakfast, if that is I could force myself to eat. Soon as I finished breakfast I'd bring my Bible with me to the hospital. I was there in time for the first visiting session of the morning and would sit and hold Julia's hand as I read her favorite scriptures from the Bible. I also read a lot from Matthew when Jesus raised Lazarus from the dead. The way I saw it, if God could do that for Lazarus he could do that for me too and bring Julia back from the dark world of the coma. I would be there for an hour just long enough to read her Scripture, talk to her briefly and make sure the nurses put food in Julia's tubes. Then I would rush to the lumber yard and work all day. During my lunch break I would call Frank and see if they had seen Julia yet and we would exchange updates if there were any, which more often than not there weren't. Some days it would look like she blinked an eyelid and I would mention it to the nurses or doctor only to have them say I must have imagined it. I can't begin to tell you how weary I grew of looking for a sign, any sign that Julia was getting better. When I'd get off work in the evenings I would go straight to the hospital and spend the night with Julia for as long as I could. Often, I would fall asleep by her bedside and a nurse would wake me up then I would force myself to leave only to return the next morning. Majority of the time when I arrived home at night I would be awake long enough to walk the dog, decide against popping a frozen dinner in the microwave and fall asleep on our bed with my work clothes still on.

Letters poured in from people I didn't even know. There were a lot of letters from people that knew Julia at college, professors and students. Covered dishes were sent to the house by various members of the congregation where Alice and Frank and recently Julia and I were members. The congregation would rotate days to cook for me. I think Alice must have told the interpreter that I don't normally cook for myself. I had no choice but to accept the food they brought. Majority of the time it went bad in the refrigerator simply because I was too exhausted to force myself to eat. I went a few times to church with Frank and Alice but it was more than enough for me. I didn't feel like I belonged anywhere without Julia.

The police never caught the boys that shot Julia and robbed the convenience store. I know I was supposed to pray for them. The pastor mentioned it the Sunday after Julia was put in a coma. He mentioned loving our enemies and blessing those that curse us. He said we should rejoice when afflicted because Christ was afflicted. But it was hard for me to shake the fact that someone had stolen my wife away from me. I punched a hole through our kitchen wall one night in a rage of anger. Our Dalmatian just stared and ran under the sofa in fear. I'd screamed at the top of my lungs and threw anything lying across the counter tops and table onto the floor. That was the night the police showed up to tell me they were giving up on finding the thieves. I felt like they were letting me down and worse yet, letting Julia down. It took time, lots of time for me to forgive the group of boys that hurt Julia. I didn't think I could find such forgiveness inside me. And I couldn't. I found it in Christ.

I blamed myself every day for the outcome of Julia's condition. It should have been me in that hospital bed lying in a coma. It should have been me taking the bullet and because of my foolish forgetfulness my wife was dying. I would have taken a bullet for her any day but the day she needed me I wasn't there. It was all my fault and I felt like everyone in the world knew it but wasn't saying it. I wished more than anything that it could have been me. I prayed for it to be me. I asked God to let me die and Julia live more times than I can count but he didn't. He let me live and I couldn't understand why. I wanted my wife back, my caring, funny, sweet wife back. But there was no trading the cards that had been dealt and I began to resent myself for that. I knew Julia wouldn't want me to blame myself. In fact, she would have spent days convincing me not to blame myself. Frank tried to convince me in her stead. It was then that I knew where Julia got her powers of persuasion from. He convinced me that what I needed to do was forgive myself. And it was a hard thing to do. Frank told me that Julia would never blame me and that she loved me.

Then finally one morning nearly five months after the initial gun shot that sent Julia into a coma, the doctor approached me and said our insurance would not cover the costs of Julia's life support anymore. He said in his best professional opinion it was time to let her go. They'd been monitoring her progress and as far as they had seen there was none. I told him I wanted a second opinion. Unfortunately our insurance would not cover moving Julia to another hospital so I had to settle for seeking the opinion of other doctors within the same hospital and the verdict remained the same. A week later I was terrified, absolutely and positively terrified. I called Frank on my cell phone and told him and Alice to come to Julia's room. There was no more money to pay for Julia's bills and we were already going into debt, both Frank and I. The church had been so kind in helping us but they were unable to help further. Frank's voice shook when I called him. He knew it was the day he would say goodbye to his daughter.

I sat in the plastic chair opposite of Julia next to the window until Frank and Alice arrived. I'd been trying to think of what to say to my wife. I wondered for the forty thousandth time if maybe she could hear me and what if once the nurse pulled the plug Julia came out of the coma gasping for air. I didn't want to be the one to do it and I couldn't bear the thought of seeing them pull the plug. I knew I wouldn't be there when the doctor came in. Julia wouldn't want me to see her that way.

My mind raced with every word Julia and I had ever exchanged. I thought of the first time we'd met, our first kiss, our first confession of love, when I proposed to her, the silly fights we'd had, our wedding day by the pond at the park, everything. But more than anything I thought of the last time I'd seen her smiling at me. I thought of the spoiled casserole on the counter that she never finished, the Aspirin I never got to set out for her headache and the stupid candles that were never lit on the dinner table. There were so many moments that we had yet to make and now we would never have them. She was too young to die. She was too innocent and pure, beautiful, sensational and intelligent. I couldn't bring myself to say goodbye. It was one of the many run from my fears sort of moments that have defined the core of my existence.

Instead I prayed for the strength to walk to her bedside, leaned over and kissed her on the lips. Her lips still felt warm, soft and moist they way they used to. I waited there with my lips over hers and our noses almost touching for a second so that

I could remember what it was like to be this close to her forever. My hand shook as I stretched it forward to run my hand through her hair. It was silky and smooth. I couldn't count how many times I had run my hand through that head of hair. It used to smell like Citrus shampoo but now it didn't. I moved my mouth near her right ear and whispered in it, "Julia, I'm so sorry. Please--" my voice shattered into a million pieces and I began to cry despite my best efforts not to.

I wanted to be strong for her because she would want me to be, "Forgive me. I love you so much, Baby, so very much'" I paused to catch my breath and looked at her, really took her in one last time. My whole being ached, "One day I will see you again." I shut my eyes and rose from the plastic chair.

I remember walking outside her room with the feeling of not being able to breathe. It felt like the weight of the world lay on my chest causing it to cave in and I was gasping for air. My heart was in shreds. I knew there were other people in the hospital dying. There were also babies being born, and none of it seemed right. Julia was about to die and I felt like I was dying at the same time. I was angry that I had to be the one to make the decision. I knew legally I had to as her husband. I also knew the doctor would come in any moment and ask me about donating Julia's organs to Science or giving to the latest person in need on the donor list so when he walked toward me I told him to talk to Julia's parents. They would donate the organs to the donor list I was sure and this is what Julia would have wanted. I just didn't want to have to deal with that right now.

I paced in the hallway until I saw Alice and Frank. Alice had a handful of used tissues in her hand and Frank's face was pale. I wondered if mine looked like that. Julia was their only child. I could never begin to understand what they were going through. Julia was irreplaceable to the three of us. I nodded at them. Alice signed to me its okay, Collin. Julia loves you. We love you. She's going to see Jesus. Frank touched me on the arm and the two of them walked into Julia's room.

The pastor followed shortly thereafter. I couldn't think straight as I saw him walk toward me. I knew he wanted to say something but I didn't want to say anything. It was fitting that he was there when she gave her life to Christ and there now that she was walking into his arms. He carried his Bible in his right hand and paused when he got to me.

He opened his mouth but I stopped him, "Please," I fought to catch my voice. It was like it was running from me, "read Matthew 11:9. It's her favorite," I whispered. He nodded and gave a halfway smile as he patted me on the back and entered Julia's room. Two nurses filed in with charts and a stop watch in their hands. All the necessary parties were there.

I leaned my back onto the wall outside her door. I turned my head to the side to hear the beeping of her machines. They still beat loudly. I couldn't make out the words in the room for the beating of my own heart. It beat rapidly and I thought about how Julia's was about to stop. I began to second guess if I had said everything I should have to her. I thought about all the times I could have been a better husband in the three months we were married. That was when I heard it. Julia's machines stopped. The mumbled voices in her room ceased. I held my breath. Julia… Then I heard a loud beep sound from her room that carried on. Tears sprung to my eyes and all I could think about was how my wife was gone. I slid down the wall and held my head in my hands. The doctor and nurses filed out the door. The pastor said something to me but I hadn't a clue what. I could hear Frank and Alice wailing in Julia's room. I knew I should go in but all I could think was *She's gone.*

CHAPTER NINE

I shifted my feet again as I thought about these things. Karen trudged down the stairs and entered the kitchen again. I knew I should say something to her. If she wanted me to apologize for still loving Julia, I couldn't. Yet I still felt guilty. I thought about how long it had been since I'd been to church. I knew they would have a night service since it was Sunday.
"I'm sorry I yelled at you," I told her. Karen stabbed her fork into the Ravioli and looked at the salad. She nodded. "I'm thinking about going to church tonight. Do you want to go with me?"
"To church?" She didn't try to hide the shock in her voice.
"Yeah, I haven't been in a while and I want to go."
"No, thanks. I'm kind of tired. I don't really feel like going." I understood. It was my fault.
Karen finished her meal shortly thereafter. I had stabbed at my food then decided I had lost my appetite so I threw mine out. Karen volunteered to do the dishes and I traversed up the steps to change for the service. She seemed puzzled when she saw me come down and realized I was serious about going to the service. I gave her a kiss on the cheek and said I'd be back before long.

The drive to the church was not as I remembered it. Lanterns surrounded the outside of the church. I wondered if Frank and Alice would be there. It had been forever since I talked to them. I'm sure the pastor would be surprised to see me. I opened up the car door and made sure I turned my cell phone off. I started to walk toward the church then halted.

It looked like... Julia. A slender blonde with apple cheeks walked up the steps to enter the church. Her stance was much like Julia's.

I had to get closer.

I knew it couldn't be Julia. She'd died four years ago. Still, I had to calm the voice inside me. I rushed toward the church steps. When I entered I saw her at the back pew. Her hair was up in a bun and she wore a scarf around her neck. She wore a denim skirt and a blue blouse. I kept staring at her as the service started. The pastor began the hymnals. The woman who looked like Julia looked back at me. I saw something in her eyes and that's when I knew. It was Julia. It had to be. I know it sounds crazy, but it was her. She rose from the pew and turned her head from my gaze in a hurry. She scurried out of the church and I followed after her. I knew I was causing uproar but I didn't care. She scurried to her car and got inside. She didn't look back. I watched her drive off.

My heart sank. Why would a woman run from me if I'd never met her and only looked at her? She wouldn't... unless she was Julia.

I didn't return to the church. I walked toward my car, unlocked it, and got in. Maybe I was imagining things like what the grief counselor said. What had he called them… hallucinations? But somehow I highly doubted that I would still be imagining things a supposed four years after Julia's death. I ran my right hand through my hair. Something wasn't adding up. My first instinct was to go to Frank and Alice's. Maybe Julia would be there, if that is, Julia was still alive. There was a nagging feeling at the back of my mind that something just wasn't right. I couldn't be certain exactly what that was but I knew it had something to do with Julia. I began to have the sickening feeling that I had been lied to these last four years.

But why? Why would Julia let me believe she were dead? That just wasn't Julia. She loved me as much as I loved her and if the tables were turned I never would have let her go on believing I were dead when I was alive.

I shoved my keys in the ignition and gunned my car after the woman who was the spitting image of Julia. I was driving seventy miles per hour in a thirty zone. If a cop were hiding behind a pair of bushes nearby I wouldn't have noticed. Her black Toyota was two cars in front of me preparing to make a left at the stop light. I swerved to the left to follow her. I think she knew I was still following her because she was driving rather recklessly. I analyzed everything about her driving. Julia had been a pretty careful driver even when she sped. The driver in front of me was too she just seemed nerved. But why unless something had taken an emotional toll on her. Something like seeing her husband again? She sped and so did I. I had questions and the uneasy feeling that she had the answers. The black Toyota gunned it through the next stop light and a car cut in front of me. She disappeared in the distance. I lost her.

Again.

I struck the steering wheel with my fists and the cars around me stared at the sight of me blaring my horn at no one in particular. I bounced my leg wondering where I should go next. I couldn't go home. If I did, I would just stare at the ceiling the entire night. I decided to head to the hospital. I'd talk to Julia's doctor and check the records to see if in fact she was dead. That would ease my concerns and if it showed she was in fact dead I could put all of this to rest. I couldn't decide if I wanted to be crazy or not.

I drove toward the hospital and paced myself to the help desk. I asked for Dr. Mathis who had been the one to handle Julia's care in her last days. The nurse looked puzzled. She said Dr. Mathis wouldn't be in until morning. Right. Of course he wouldn't be in when I needed him. That would be too easy. I thanked her and left the hospital more disappointed now than when I first began my search. My brain toyed with ways I could search for the truth. And then it hit me. The graveyard. I could check the local grave yard. There was only one is Sea Breeze and Frank and Alice had planned to bury her there.

I cranked my ignition and headed along the

dark road toward the grave yard. It was on the outskirts of town and I must confess I hadn't been there since my grandmother died. I didn't go to Julia's funeral. I knew I should have. I could only imagine what people said about me not going but I couldn't face it. Like I said, I made a habit of running from the difficult things to avoid them. It was a rainy day when they supposedly buried Julia and I had had nightmares that night about her beautiful body rising to the top of the grave from the rain that had created such a downpour in the town. I turned into the nearest parking space and got out of the vehicle. There were no lights out and it was incredibly hard to see. Everyone had said it would be best to forget. I began to wonder whether they were right or wrong as I walked along the gravestones. But they didn't know Julia and they certainly did not know me. I searched for the F's for Flannigan. She would be listed as Julia Douglas Flannigan. I walked slowly, afraid that I would miss her tombstone. I could hear the crunch of the leaves beneath my shoes. The night swirled around me and a faint breeze picked up and hit my back. It reminded me of the first day I met Julia the weather had been much like this. Then I saw it.

Her tombstone was there: Julia Douglas Flannigan, her birth date was listed but there was no date of death. No flowers placed on the grave. Nothing. Apparently I paid for a tombstone that had only been partially chiseled. I squinted my eyes at the tombstone and double checked it just to make sure I wasn't imagining things. Nope.

Julia Douglas Flannigan 1983-

I kicked at the grass on her supposed grave. Her body wasn't here. I knew that now. The question was if Julia's body wasn't here, where was it?

CHAPTER TEN

That night I had drove home in a trance. By the time I came in Karen was already in bed. I knew she wouldn't be pleased that I'd stayed out so late. It seemed I couldn't do anything right lately. I brushed my teeth and slid into the bed in my boxers. I wasn't tired. I couldn't sleep. The event of the night replayed itself in my mind.

Karen slid her arm around me and rubbed her hand over my abs. I squeezed her arm to let her know I noticed her. She didn't say anything. She rubbed my abs again. This time I ignored it. She leaned toward me and nudged her nose at my shoulder. I laid there. She sighed and rolled over on top of me, slowly. She kissed my arm and trailed her way up my neck. She stopped when she got to my ear.

"Karen, not tonight honey."

She said nothing. I knew she was a time bomb waiting to explode. She wanted to know why. I couldn't provide the answer. She wouldn't like it if I did.

Karen rolled off me and turned her back to me. I heard her sigh as her head hit the pillow again. "I love you," she said.

The next weekend I was supposed to go canoeing with Alvin, my eldest brother. We hadn't gone canoeing since I was five and he was eight years old. Mom had still been alive and Dad had been quite the sports enthusiast. Alvin took me by surprise when he called me at the firm to say he wanted to go canoeing again. When I told Karen about it she was supportive and encouraged me to go spend time with my brother. I couldn't help but question if she had introduced the idea to Alvin in the first place. It was no matter to me. I wanted to get away for a while and spend some time out on the water.

It was about ten o' clock by the time we pushed the rental canoe out on the water. Alvin had packed an ice chest full of beer and other assortments. I had brought the sun block and fishing rods in case we decided to test our chances out on the water. He didn't say much. He asked the basics: how's the wife, the job, the life. Fine, I told him. We sat in silence rowing the paddles in the water. The creek had begun to look much like a swamp with moss hanging from the old trees. Stumps were strewn in the water from the hurricane two years ago, which made it difficult to maneuver the canoe around the limbs. If I listened closely I could hear crickets behind the trees on the bayou and the mosquitoes dancing on the water. Obviously the hurricane from two years ago still had the crickets confused. Every now and then a turtle would poke its head up out of the water only to dive under it again once he saw the canoe. The sky was a strange purple and blue. We'd seen a few canoes pass us by along the way, but not many. We'd been on the water rowing for about two hours when I was studying the sky more closely. I inhaled the air and closed my eyes. Something about this place was peaceful.

Peculiar, but peaceful. I should come here more often, I thought. Then I brought my eyes back to the water and that's when I saw her.

She was in a canoe being rowed by some guy in a blue baseball cap and shorts. She was wearing a green swimsuit top and a swimsuit scarf around her bottoms. As she drew closer I could see freckles on her shoulders and a fresh tan on her skin. Her hair hung carelessly and brushed her shoulders. When she turned her head, it was then that she saw me. I began to wonder if she was even breathing. She began to breathe deep and didn't take her eyes off me. I tried not to blink. I was hallucinating, wasn't I? This was just another bad dream and I wondered if any minute now I would wake up to a world without her in it. I parted my lips to catch more air in my lungs. I had to breathe, needed to remember to breathe. It felt like someone had hurled a sword in my chest. Julia's violet eyes pierced mine. Something sad hung behind them. There was no doubt in my mind.

It was Julia.

Alvin began to row slowly. I knew he was thinking the same thing. I stood up in the canoe and shouted at her when she was about twenty feet from our canoe, "Julia!" The canoe rocked beneath me. My knees buckled. She flinched and her eyebrows dropped. Her mouth parted in surprise and it looked to me like she was shivering. It was warm enough outside to prevent that from happening. She was shivering because it was me. That was my answer.

I didn't bother to kick off my sandals. Instead, I dove straight into the water, unaware of the turtles and fish that might nibble on my toes. When I dove in, I accidentally inhaled some bayou water and came up spitting. Julia clung to the side of her canoe and watched me swim toward her. I swam as fast as I could. The water was cool against my upper body. I could feel it seeping into my swim trunks. I lost my sandals beneath the water. When I approached the side of the canoe I hoisted myself into it and rolled over onto my side, coughing up water. The canoe wavered back and forth with my tumble into it. I was out of breath and my chest heaved for air. Julia stood then and helped pull me up. It looked like she was in shock. The man in the canoe with us was growing irate.

"Julia, do you know this man?" He shouted with irritation fresh in his voice.

I stretched forward my wet hands and cradled her face. It was her.

She searched my eyes and pressed her hands to my wet chest. "He's my husband," Julia breathed.

CHAPTER ELEVEN

"What are you doing here?" I could have thought of a million other questions to ask her but that was the first one to untangle itself from my lips.
"It's a long story," Julia shook her head and took a seat at the front of the canoe. She faced me as her eyes raced over me. I knew she was taking me in to see if I'd changed. Her eyes rested on my abs. They weren't as great as they once had been when I worked at the lumber yard, but they were still pretty solid. She bit her lip and looked away with flushed cheeks once she realized I knew what she was doing.
"I've got time," I told her with a sudden burst of anger wrestling in my chest, "It's been four years, Julia. I thought you were dead."
She hung her head and focused her sight on the floor of the canoe, "I know. Look," She raised her eyes to meet mine and I know I wouldn't win the struggle to keep my emotions in check, "there's a lot to say but we'll have to wait until we dock."
"How long?" I asked the guy behind us steering the canoe.
"Five minutes," He piped.

I sighed and pulled Julia into my arms. I wrapped my arms around her and squeezed her tight. She leaned her head on my shoulder and her body shook. I took my index finger and wiped a tear from her eye. It had been so long, so very long since I had held her.

Everything came rushing to me at once. My wife was alive. She was in my arms. I was married to Karen, sure, but there was no one to me that came close in comparison to my love for Julia. God had answered my prayers when I thought he hadn't heard me. She was alive, she was well and we could have our second chance.

I swallowed hard as we approached the dock and the man steering pulled the equipment out of the canoe. I helped Julia out of the canoe and onto the bank. She pulled a couple of bills and thrust the money at the man. He grunted and pulled the canoe onto a trailer connected to a truck. He left a few minutes later.

I was frozen and began to wonder if I could even talk.

"Follow me," She said. And I did.

Julia led me to a cabin near the bayou. She unlocked the wooden door and pushed it open. There was a light on the front of the cabin. The shutters were painted black and on the side of the cabin was the black Toyota I saw earlier at the church. She led the way into the cabin and turned on the light at the door. She tossed her coin purse onto a tiny sofa to the right and offered me a drink. I declined. She waited for a few seconds as though unsure what to say to me. She disappeared into the next room and returned with an old towel. I thanked her and spread it on the sofa so I wouldn't soak it too horribly. Julia studied me again. I watched her eyes dance along my chest, my arms, my abs and stop at my waist. She looked to the hand I had grabbed the towel with and stared at it. I cleared my throat and she looked away. She'd seen my wedding band.

Julia pressed her lips together and took a few steps toward me. She sat down next to me. She swallowed hard and stared straight ahead. I scooted closer to her and put my arm around her. She shook her head and tears began to pour. I tried to wipe them away but she pushed my hands away. I was taken aback by her independence and wondered what had caused it. She'd been through something I could never identify with. It hurt to watch her sit next to me and not allow me to help her.

She inhaled and began, "I want you to know that I made every effort to find you."
"And I you," I said quickly.
"Collin, just let me say this so you can leave."

My eyebrows jumped. What was she talking about leave? It had been four years and now she wanted her say so I could leave? It took all I had to be patient and listen without budding in. But I wanted to know, had to know what happened. She was being sharp with me and I had a terrible feeling that whatever she had been through was a result of me.

Julia focused on her hands that were clasped together. She leaned her elbows on her knees then opened her mouth, "You thought I was dead. Dr. Mathis had the nurses unplug me. They thought it would be a normal procedure. But it wasn't. Minutes later I gasped for breath and the machines went off. I was fighting to breathe and my body was going into shock. They rushed in and hooked me up to the machines again. When they did, they were able to limit the amount of life support I was on. It looked like I was breathing on my own so they took me off again.

"I breathed shallowly for days. They monitored me thinking I would die on my own. They tried to call you but you didn't answer. So they called my parents. They came and Dr. Mathis told them he'd never seen anything like this before. I woke up one day not knowing where I was or what was going on. I couldn't remember anything. This lasted for months and I do mean months.

"Mom wanted to contact you to let you know, but when she did a woman answered the phone. When she asked who she was the woman said she was your wife,"

Here Julia stared me in the eye and continued, "You had moved on. She told me you were married but I couldn't believe it. I had to see it for myself. I looked you up in the phone book and saw you listed at the local firm so I placed a call there. Your secretary answered and said you weren't in. She asked if I was a friend of yours and

I said yes. She told me you were out with your wife and that you were expecting a baby…" Julia clasped her hand over her mouth and tried to catch her breath.

"I told her not to say anything to anyone. She never listens," I gritted my teeth and reached my hand toward her, "Karen's not pregnant."
"So that's her name," Julia nodded and continued. I wanted to slap myself. "I waited a few days and decided to drive by the house I had an address for. You were outside washing your car and I saw Karen…," she tried out her name for the first time, "bringing you something to drink. You looked happy together. I thought how presumptuous it was of me that you would wait for your dead wife to come home. I was a fool. I should have known you would move on. I should have known not to drive by your house," Julia sucked in her breath and when her eyes looked in mine they were red, "I drove off before you could see me. I've been here ever since. I couldn't go back to the school and work there. I wasn't the same person anymore, not after everything I'd seen. I applied for a school just outside Sea Breeze and began working there as a school nurse."

I looked around and saw there was nothing personal in the cabin. There were no pictures of friends or family. No pink things. There were no paintings on the walls. Just a television along the wall, a small gas stove in the kitchen, and an even smaller wooden table by a window in the corner with two chairs tucked under it.

I thought of how lonely she must have been in this place. I thought about how lonely I was even with someone else living under my roof. I thought of all the time we could have spent together if only I had known she was alive. I was angry with her and I knew I had a right to be. I was angry with her parents, the doctors, the nurses, angry with everyone. But more than anything I just wanted to be with her again and forget the four years that had separated us. There was a familiar ache that increased all the more when I looked at Julia. I wanted to kiss her so badly and make our pain go away. I was the villain in her story. I was the one that had moved on and taken a wife. I was sickened when I thought of all the hurt I caused her and all the times I made love to Karen when I could have made love to Julia. I wondered if she had seen anyone else, and if she was now.

"I know there is nothing I can say or do to change what has happened. I'm so sorry for everything. If I had known you were alive I never would have remarried. I always loved you. I still do," Her eyes grew when I made that statement and suddenly I became embarrassed, "But just answer me this, please," Julia looked to me, confused that I was making an apology, "Do you still love me?" My voice shook and at first I wondered if Julia had even heard me.

She rose from the sofa and walked toward the kitchen but stopped before she reached it. She placed her hands on her hips and looked toward the floor. It was like she was weighing something in the back of her mind. For the first time ever, the thought occurred to me that perhaps she didn't love me anymore and that terrified me more than anything. I was absolutely petrified that she might not love me anymore and that I was in this alone.

I tried again, "Julia, do you love me?"
I thought I heard her begin to cry but I couldn't be sure. I rose from the sofa and trekked toward her. I outstretched my hand and began to reach for her. She swirled around, tears hot and stinging in her eyes, "Yes Collin, I do. Very much," Her voice was so soft I almost didn't hear it. Then her voice rose to a scream and I wanted to jump back, "But that doesn't change a thing! You're married Collin you're married! You have a wife and she isn't me! Do you think everything can just magically go back to the way it used to be? After all this time we can just snap our fingers and poof everyone is alright?" She approached me and I grabbed her by the arms.
"You're my wife."
Julia furiously shook her head, "Not anymore, Collin. Not anymore. I'm dead, remember?" She tried to pull away from me but I wouldn't let her go. "Let me go," She commanded.
"Not a chance."
She tried to release herself from my grip again.

"What did you expect me to do? Just waltz up to your doorstep and say 'Hello Collin, hi Collin's wife, I'm his wife he thought was dead and I just thought I'd let you know?' What, that you'd divorce her? Marriage is sacred, Collin. I don't believe in divorce and neither do you…"
"I know. I don't know what I thought…"
"That's right, you don't know. How do you think I felt knowing you were with her every single night?" Julia brought her hand to her chest and hit it hard, "Don't you think it hurt me? Don't you think I died inside?"
"Julia," I forced her to look at me, by guiding her jaw with my finger, "I wanted to believe you were alive but everyone told me I was in shock. They sent me to grief counseling. I wanted you but I couldn't have you. You were dead. I had this poison inside me eating me alive. I was dying inside too. Do you have any idea how much I missed you? Hell, I still miss you."

She pounded at my chest then and I pulled her closer. She sobbed onto my chest and her knees began to buckle. I held her up and brought her back to the sofa. I placed her in my lap and wrapped her in my arms. She cried for a long time, for what seemed like an hour. I didn't say anything. I held her tightly. It was like I was afraid to loosen my grip to find that she wasn't really alive and I was living a dream. I stroked her hair and pulled the towel from under me to let her blow her nose and wipe her eyes. Julia held on tightly to my stomach. I could feel her breath on my skin. Her tears were warm on me.

"I saw you at the church," She sniffled, "but I couldn't say anything. I just ran."
"I know," I held her tighter.
"I didn't know what to say. How could I? I knew you would blame yourself for everything if you knew. I knew we could never be together again. I knew all that. So I ran." Running was one thing I knew a lot about.
"I've been running from my love for you for way too long. But it looks like my shadow finally caught up to me," I stroked Julia's cheek and she looked up into my eyes. I wouldn't leave her again.

CHAPTER TWELVE

I half expected Alvin to call me. I definitely expected Karen to call. But she didn't. It was then that I knew Alvin had told her what happened. I didn't know what my move would be once I left Julia's place for home. I didn't have one. There was no manual on what to do when your wife is resurrected from the dead.

Julia changed into a t-shirt and shorts. We drove down to the local store and she picked me out some plaid shorts and a t-shirt. Neither one of us were crazy about them, but there wasn't much to choose from there and we didn't want to venture too far. We had four years of lost time to catch up on. Once we got back to Julia's she pulled some defrosted ground beef from the refrigerator and cooked it in a skillet on the stove. She pulled the rest of the ingredients for spaghetti and placed them on the counter. She had always been a delicious cook, which was why I never had to learn to cook anything fancy. I watched her cut the chives with ease and studied her even more closely. She looked the same as she did when I'd seen her last. Her cheeks were like blushing apples and her skin was smooth and creamy. Her lips were a bright red from being out in the sun and her hair brushed across her shoulders like a gentle wave. She had developed bicep muscles since I'd seen her last and I wondered how she got them.

Was she into Karate now? Did she frequent the gym?

It occurred to me that I knew nothing about her anymore and that just a few hours spent with her would never suffice. Julia lifted her head to see me studying her and smiled. I walked toward her and put my arms around her waist as she tossed the chives into the pot on the stove. As she continued cooking I rested my chin on her shoulder and kissed her there.

"I could ruin dinner with you doing that," She said with a laugh. It was the first time I'd heard her laugh in four years and it took me aback. I'd forgotten just how good it sounded. I pulled my head away slightly, surprised at hearing it then smiled. I brought my nose to her hair and breathed in the scent of Citrus. Her hair smelt like Citrus, just like I remembered only it smelt better this time, if possible. I wanted to kiss her but knew I couldn't.

"Why don't you get a shower? I have plenty of soap and shampoo in the tub. Towels are under the sink. And you have to be careful with the water when you turn it on because sometimes the handle wants to fall off…" Julia turned to look at me then realized I'd been staring at her again. "Here," she said as she pushed past me and led me to the bathroom, "I'll just show you," She opened the shower curtain then turned the hot water knob.

I noted how slender she still was as she leaned

over to turn the water on. Her body had always been shaped like an hour glass. It still was. She kicked her right foot up ever so slightly as the twisted the knob. I couldn't believe I'd forgotten things like that about her.
"Julia," I took her hand and pulled her to me, "I want nothing more than to kiss you right now. To just be here with you like it used to be but I can't." Her eyes grew and she put her index finger to my mouth to shut me up, "I know."
I shook my head, "No, you don't. There is so much we have missed. I wish I could take it all back and make up for lost time…" I lifted her chin with my finger and traced it.

    She looked like she was afraid to move. I brought my lips to her forehead and kissed it, then her left cheek, her right cheek, her chin, and her nose. We brushed noses and she smiled. She instinctively brought her right hand to the top button on my shirt then paused.

    If I didn't get her out of here soon something would happen. I released her then and she left the bathroom without saying a word. The bathroom smelt like lavender.

    While I took a shower I questioned whether too much time had elapsed for Julia and I to ever truly know each other again. It seemed like decades ago and yet strangely enough it felt like it was just yesterday that she stepped out the door and left my life forever. I knew I was different. I now worked at a law firm. I had somehow lost hold of living life for the beauty of it instead of being boring and predictable. It seemed I was following in my father's footsteps after all. Julia was in the career she had intended as a school nurse though her life had not gone as planned.

As I stepped out of the shower I put my weight on something exceptionally fuzzy. A brown cat shrieked and ran behind the toilet. I scratched my wet hair and wondered when Julia had gotten a cat. She used to love dogs when we were together. When I came out she was nearly finished cooking supper.

"Since when do you like cats? " I hadn't intended to blurt it out like I did but there it was.
Julia laughed and pushed back a strand of hair that fell in her face. "Who, Melrose? " I shrugged like I used to when Julia and I first met. "Oh, he's harmless. He's afraid of any new thing or person. Dad found him outside his office as a kitten and brought him home. Mom didn't want him so I took him in. I missed having Eddy around… well, and you. I needed some company so I took him in. It was either that or the pound. I didn't have the heart to turn him away," Here she sighed, "it's not the same as having you or Eddy around but not much is since the accident," Julia placed two empty glasses on the counter and searched through the cabinet to her left, "Whatever happened to Eddy?" She meant our Dalmatian. "He misses you, but who can blame him," She smiled as if to say No, really, so I said, "He's

good."

I walked into the kitchen and reached over her to grab a bag of tea. When I pulled it out I saw that it was Mango. It felt like a brick hit my chest. Of course she had Mango tea. It was still Julia's favorite. "Do you know," I said, "that I was determined once you came home from the grocery store that night to sit you out some Advil for your headache light some candles for a romantic dinner and make you your favorite drink?" I held up the packet of tea, "Mango Tea." I tore open the wrapper and dropped the tea bag in the tea maker.

"You remembered?" I witnessed something sad again behind Julia's eyes.

"Of course, "I saddled up to her and she put her hand to my cheek. I was surprised by her affection and let it rest there.

She rubbed her index finger along my cheek and gave a little tug on my shirt. "What do you miss the most?" She asked. I stood there unable to limit the beauty of our past life together into one moment. "Do you know what I miss the most?" I shook my head. She leaned in closer to me and whispered in my ear, "Waking up next to you every morning in my arms," Julia cuddled on me then.

"This is all my fault," I told her.

"What do you mean?" She pulled away for a moment to look at me.

"If only I had gotten the milk. And what were you thinking trying to stop those thieves? You could have ever ventured far.

Julia pulled herself away from cuddling at my chest, "Oh don't start with that. This is not your fault. And what did you expect me to do just stand there and watch them rob the store owner blind? Someone had to do something." Julia's arms flailed.

"You're not Superwoman, Julia," I stopped, hoping to prevent an argument, "Just promise me you will never go for milk again. I'll go."

"How can you?" I furrowed my eyebrows and she replied, "You're married, remember."

Her words pierced me and I fought to keep my senses, "Like I said, this is all my fault. If I would have remembered to purchase the milk, if I would have been in the room when they unplugged you, if I had answered the phone when the doctor called, if I hadn't remarried…" I let out some hot air through my teeth, "There are a hundred things I would have done differently but none of them will give me you," I bunched up my fist and was ready to swing at the wall. Julia stopped me.

"We can either beat ourselves up over this and get nowhere or we can move on," She released my arm and placed dinner on the small wooden table by the window.

I knew it was just as hard for her to face this as it was for me, but Julia seemed to be taking it better. Perhaps that was because she knew everything I had just learned this afternoon for four years and had time to meditate on it.

We ate dinner in silence for quite a while until Julia lifted her glass of Mango tea to finish it off. She pursed her lips like she was measuring the weight of all that she was about to say then wavered as though unsure she should reveal anything.

There was a burning in my chest and it wasn't from the food. The longer I was near her the more it felt like a fire was consuming me. There was so much I wanted to know that I didn't even know where to begin. I sat my fork in the middle of my plate and started to mop the condensation from my glass and gather my napkin then stopped myself. If I didn't ask her now, I never would.

I swallowed hard, "Tell me about yourself."
Julia leaned back in her chair as though uncertain what I meant, "What do you mean?"
"It's been four years. I can't even begin to imagine what happened in that time frame," My eyes grazed the table, "I've changed. I'm sure you must have too."
"Changed? Oh," Julia waved a hand in the air as if she were dismissing the idea of it, "I haven't changed that much, have I?"
"No," I said quickly, "You're still mesmerizing. And beautiful." I figured I must have been out of line but I could have sworn I saw her blush.
Julia chose to overlook the compliment. I knew it was more from nervousness than anything, "You look good too," She looked me hard in the eyes then. It felt like she was seeping into my soul with

her eyes. "Well," She said changing the subject, "I joined a kick boxing class," She saw my eyes pop so she went on, "Yeah! Yeah, I know… Me in kick boxing. Who would have thought?," Julia leaned forward and placed her elbows on the table. She propped her chin in to one of her hands, "The instructor says I show great promise. I've been doing it for two years and I absolutely love it. "
"You always were full of fire."
She laughed at that and continued, "I even started lifting weights to build up my arms so that my legs wouldn't be the only thing in shape."
"So that explains the biceps."
"Oh, you saw those, huh?" She wrinkled her nose. "You want to hear more? "
"Please," I was enjoying watching her animated face light up talking about those things. I could watch her the whole night.
"I volunteer as a sort of counselor for deaf children and their parents. Mom works at the Center helping the children. She told me about a volunteer position they had available so I took it. It is the most rewarding thing I have ever done. I get to help deaf children and their parents bond. There is this wall between the two worlds and I get to tear it down so they can begin to understand each other better." Julia tapped her fingertips on the wooden table like she used to do when she was excited.
"Wow."
"What?"
"You're really doing it," I said, clearing my throat.

"You're living your dream. Your parents must be really proud of you. I know I am, for what it's worth."

"No, it means a lot to me actually," Julia fidgeted with her napkin on the table. Without meeting my eyes she said, "I'm living the dream yes, but I always thought it would be with you."

I nodded, afraid to see what might be in her eyes if I looked at them, "I did too."

She heaved a heavy sigh then said, "So tell me about you. Four years can be a lifetime." It troubled me to hear her say that. Had it felt like a lifetime to her? "Tell me about your life. I want to know everything."

I looked to her as though to say 'Really?'

"Yes," Julia gave me a daring look, "really!"

"Alright then. The good, bad or the ugly version?"

"All of it. I have the rest of the evening," Julia twirled her glass on the table then brought her hand back to her lap.

I smiled, grateful for her interest. It took a lot for her to say that considering the things I could say that could unintentionally hurt her, like mentioning Karen, for instance. "Um…" I struggled to find something interesting to say about my life then decided to just give the raw version, "I run a lot."

"As do I."

"I never doubted as much. After you left I ran even more. My family, shockingly enough, thought I'd run myself mad. Dr. Mathis thought I ought to see a grief counselor," I saw Julia swallow hard, "I used to feel you in the night lying next to me and in the morning I could smell your perfume," I thought I saw Julia's eyes begin to water but I continued anyway. It had been a long time and I desired for her to know the truth. I wanted her to know her love for me had not been in vain and that for what it was worth, I did miss her terribly. "I even thought I heard your voice while I was walking Eddy or washing dishes." Julia cupped her hand over her mouth. I leaned on the table, "Julia," I said more a whisper than anything, "I never wanted to believe you were gone. But the counselor told me I was in shock and it was hallucinations. He said it was part of the grief process and I had to let you go. But I couldn't let you go, Julia. I haven't and I still can't."

Julia wiped a free tear with the back of her hand and looked away. A wave of silence passed between us then she asked, "Do you still work at the lumber yard?"

"No," I said much to my own disappointment, "I don't. Karen thought I ought to put my law degree to use and I didn't want to disappoint her so I applied at the firm and got in. It was easier than I wanted it to be. In many ways after your death I felt like I had to grow up. People expected me to move on so I did my best to keep up appearances." I ran a finger along the edge of the wooden table.

"How…?"

"Did we meet?" Julia nodded. I answered uneasily, "Many months after I thought you were gone I was still working at the lumber yard. Karen was transferred there as the new secretary. We didn't talk much at first then she eventually asked me out." I could tell Julia had heard more than her share on Karen so I changed the subject. "I'm not thrilled about my job, especially when I remember what you said."

"What exactly did I say?" Julia countered.

"It was the first day we met and you were doctoring me up. You said I should be with who makes me happy and do what makes me happy."

Julia bit her lip, "That's right. I did say that..."

"Do you still believe it?"

"Yes," She answered carefully, "but not to the detriment of others. One way I've changed is I have learned to see things in a new manner. Not everything is as black and white as it used to be. Sometimes it is blurred together and grey. Life can be complicated and things get sticky. I just try to keep a clear head and my knees on the floor in prayer."

"I stopped going to church," I blurted out. "That night I saw you was the first time I'd been since before you died."

"Why?"

I shrugged. "It was too painful. You were the reason I knew Jesus as my Savior to begin with. To me you were in the church, in every church. I just couldn't do it." I studied her then. "You're stronger than me." She gave me an incredulous look. "No, really Julia. You are. You've managed to push past all that's happened. You are actually thriving."

"I don't know if I would call this thriving…" Julia faltered.

"It's more than I've done. I liked that about you. You made things look easy."

She scoffed. "Oh, sure." She looked me in the eye then said, "It was hard for me to leave my school and go to a new one after the accident. Everything was difficult. I couldn't be me anymore. If I was, you would know I was alive and I would risk hurting you. I couldn't have that so I had to let my old life die. My friends, majority of my family, my work… all of it.

"Sometimes I still miss it, but I tell myself I'm doing the right thing by protecting you and allowing you to at least attempt to be happy," She paused here then saw I was about to speak so rushed to keep me quiet., "I like the new school I'm at. It's an even smaller town than Sea Breeze so everyone is really close. It's not so bad. I'm friends at work with some of the teachers. Some of them are in my kick boxing class. That's how I discovered it."

As Julia talked I found myself yearning to be a part of her life. I knew I could never be. She knew she could never be a part of mine again. But yet the desire still remained. We were intricately connected like the weaving in a basket. The bits and pieces of fiber that made up who we are were attached to each other. It seemed my entire life had served its purpose in leading me to Julia and there was a divine hand in reuniting us even for a short while.

I offered to clean the kitchen and do the dishes while Julia took a shower. She threw Melrose from his hiding spot in the bathroom.

The cat sauntered toward me with a sway in his step. He stopped at my feet and meowed at me. I knew he was wondering what I was doing there. Heck, I was wondering what I was doing there. I knew I should leave. As a matter of fact I knew a thousand things but it didn't do me much good because for the first time since I can remember my feet were filled with led.

I filled one side of the sink with warm water and squirted some liquid soap into it. On the other side I filled a small amount of warm water to rinse the dishes off with. Julia had an old dish rack on the counter, I noticed. The cabin was an old style which meant no dish washer. I didn't mind washing the dishes by hand. It provided something to keep my mind busy. If only I had something to calm my nerves. I was drying the last dish when Julia entered the kitchen and placed her hands on her hips.

"Come with me," She said.

I followed in her tracks. She led me to the sofa in the living room and turned on the gas for the fire place. The blue flames burst forth then burned further to display the yellow and orange. It reminded me of lava. I thought about all the places in the world I could be right now. But I was here with Julia. There was no other place I wished to be. Julia sat on the sofa and hugged her legs to her chest. She wrapped her arms around them and smiled.

She'd always loved fires. On our honeymoon we'd gone skiing at a lodge in New Mexico. There was a horrible blizzard on our last day there. It was so bad that we didn't venture out and thought we'd be forced to stay another night. Neither one of us minded. We spent the majority of the last day of our honeymoon sipping hot cocoa in front of the fireplace playing cards and snuggling.

"Do you ever blame God for this? " I asked her, seemingly out of nowhere. I wanted to know where her faith stood today.
"No," she said, "Never. It was God who gave me you in the first place. How can I be angry for that. I am happy for what we shared. The Lord gives and the Lord takes away. Who am I to question him?" I ventured toward her and sat beside her. Julia leaned her head on my shoulder. Soon her eyes were closing.

She fell asleep with her head on my shoulder. I lifted her into my arms and carried her into her bedroom.

Her room was typical with white walls and a blue comforter on her bed. She had a metal bed frame and what I assumed were gifts from the children at her school on a small wall by her closet. By her nightstand was a small picture in a frame. I laid Julia on her bed then picked up the frame. It was a picture of us. The only picture in her entire house was of us. It was taken just a few weeks before Julia was shot. She'd snapped a picture of us at the local aquarium and made a copy for both of us. She kept it in her wallet. It must have still been there the day of the accident because this one looked a little worn. I wished I could give her a copy of a better one.

Seeing the picture of us there meant the world to me. It gave me hope that maybe someday things could be the way I felt they should me. God had never desired to bring us together to separate us later. I knew that much. I surveyed her room some more and noticed a large cross over her bed. It was then that I recalled seeing a cross in every room of her cabin. Julia's faith in Christ was beautiful and strong. She had more reason to blame God than anyone for the situation she found herself in. But she didn't. Instead, she chose to thank him for what she was given and chose to make the best of her situation as she could. She wasn't walking around licking her wounds. No, she was helping others and trusting God to heal her heart. I considered whether I had ever truly surrendered my hurt to God. Was that the reason I was never able to move on? I knew my inability to move forward had been because Julia was alive and I loved her, but a part of me also knew that if I were being truly honest with myself I hadn't surrendered my pain to God. I was afraid to hand over anything else to him once he took Julia away from me.

I lay next to Julia and drifted to sleep shortly thereafter. That night we fell asleep in each other's arms and I've never been as happy as I was in those few stolen moments that ended all too quickly.

I woke once to go to the bathroom in the middle of the night and heard Julia screaming my name from the bedroom. She was sweating up a storm. I rushed over to her and held her in my arms.

"It's just a bad dream," I said, "I'm here. I didn't leave."

I had to lay down with her then. I looked her in the eyes and she stared straight back at me until she fell asleep again. I grabbed her blanket and spread it over her body. During the night my hands felt for her. With my arms, I pulled her toward me. She snuggled in my embrace. Nothing had ever felt so natural.

But now it was morning. I wanted to ravage her inch by inch, take all day pouring myself into her and proving my love. As the internal war fought within me again, Julia began to stir. Just like years ago I found myself captivated by her beauty. I could scarcely move.

CHAPTER THIRTEEN

"Collin," Julia said when she opened her eyes.

"Hmm?" I opened mine.

"You know I love you," She stretched out her hand and played with my hair.

"Good because I love you."

"Collin, this is serious," The tone in her voice took me off guard. She lifted her head from the pillow. I waited for her to continue. "We can't see each other anymore."

"What?" I shrieked.

"It's not right."

"There are a lot of things that aren't right with this scenario and they all start with you and I should be together," I sat up in the bed and looked at my clothes I bought yesterday. It seemed like the time we spent together in the past twenty-four hours had suddenly slipped away.

"But at what cost?" Julia monitored my expression, "You have a wife who loves you and you obviously love her or else you never would have married her…"

"Not like I love you! It's nothing like that!" She was trying to get rid of me.

"As much as I hate to admit it, you do," Julia turned away from me then and I turned her face toward mine again.

"I didn't know you were alive or else I never would have married her."

"It's not right for us to be together, Collin, not

like this. I wanted you to be happy and know that you were okay. And you are. That's what I want for you." Julia chewed on her bottom lip.

"Do I look okay to you?" I shot out of the bed.

"Listen to me," Julia sat on her feet on the bed. She looked defeated and her voice shook, "You have no idea how much I treasure seeing you again. You stay with me. No matter where I go or what I do you are with me. And I'm with you. I love you and I always will but this can't be. It has to be goodbye. It's not that I want it to be, but it must be."

"How can you say that?" I was outraged.

"Don't fight this, Collin."

"I wished that you were alive for four years, four years, Julia, and now that you are here you expect me to just give up?" Tears were pouring down her eyes and she shook her head. I continued anyway, "No. I won't do it." I left her bedroom in search of my swimsuit from yesterday. She followed me to the bathroom where I found my swim suit and watched me gather my things in the living room. I stopped what I was doing and looked at her, I mean really looked at her. "Have you…" I stopped short, unable to finish the question. It seemed so out of place now but I needed to know. The question had plagued me since I first saw her again.

"No," she said, "there's never been anyone else," Julia opened the front door and leaned against the wall, "Don't try to find me, Collin because you won't. I've gotten pretty good at disappearing these past four years." She pushed a strand of hair behind her ears.

"I wish you would have told me. Do you know how angry that makes me?" Julia remained silent. "I don't think God would bring you back to me only to take you away again. He wouldn't do that."

She reached up and grabbed my hand, "I remember you reading to me. I remember you saying goodbye," She saw the surprise on my face, "Thank you."

I dropped my things on the floor and took hold of her by the waist. I pulled her to me, "I will see you again. I will," I released her from my arms and leaned over to pick up my things. "I'll miss you," I said as I walked out the door. I could have sworn I heard her say "I'll miss you too." But I wouldn't know because I didn't look back.

CHAPTER FOURTEEN

I couldn't go home. Not yet anyway. I moved the clutch into its appropriate gear and shifted again. There was a terrible heat wave outside. Children ventured to the bayou. They held their parents hands as they crossed the street. I slowed down to let them pass on the road. There was a blonde girl about six or seven years old holding her father's hand. She looked a lot like I imagined Julia to have been at that age. She was adventurous and ready to submerge herself in the murky water. I needed to see Julia's parents. Frank and Alice had kept her from me for far too long to deny me face time now.

I fought to keep a few tears in check as I continued to drive down the old gravel road. I sucked it up then caught sight of myself in the rear view mirror. Julia would have said I looked atrocious. My eyes looked blood shot and my nose could pass for blistered. Though I'd slept like a baby last night I wore no evidence of it today.

I leaned my head back on the head rest and thought about Julia's words. Don't try to find me, Collin. You won't. I've gotten pretty good at disappearing these past four years. First I hadn't been there for her when I should have and now she wanted me to bail. I'd spent my life running from everyone and everything that could possibly hurt me. Now that I was determined to not run again, Julia wanted me to. Still, I knew there was sound wisdom in Julia's request. God would never have me cheat on my wife and that is what Karen is... my wife. I hadn't just made a commitment to Karen; I'd made a commitment to God. I needed to trust in him. Trust him. *Lean not unto your own understanding but in all your ways acknowledge him and he shall direct your path.* That was a word to meditate on.

I heaved a heavy sigh wondering where in the world God would have us go. I needed to believe that God knew best and I didn't. I need to have a heart like Julia's and accept his will for my life no matter what it may be and no matter the cost. Maybe one day God would reunite Julia and I again, maybe not. Maybe I would always be married to Karen. It mattered to me but I knew in the long run it didn't matter in the scheme of things. Nothing I did could make it any better. I had to learn to find contentment in God like I had the summer I came to him and not in others. My heart ached, I will give you that, but it couldn't be any more painful than what Christ endured on Calvary.

I killed the ignition once in Frank in Alice's driveway. They were home. Alice peeked out the window. When she saw my car her eyes grew and she threw the curtain back into place. I imagined her running toward the front door eager to ascertain what exactly I was doing there. I remained in my seat for a minute before exiting the vehicle. Everything looked the same as it had when I had last been here, save the new shrubs that were planted at the front of the house just before the front door.

I tried to pace myself to their front door but the closer I came to it the faster my legs carried me. I gave one sound knock and twisted the knob to open the door. It flew open before I could thrust it open.

Alice stood before me with her arms open wide. Her eyes were pleading with me. Forgive me, she signed. I thought I'd misunderstood especially since it had been so long for me to be around ASL. Forgive me, she signed again. I nodded. Alice tapped on the wall behind her to get Frank's attention wherever he was. She tapped hard on the wall again. I rushed past her to look for Frank myself. I found him sitting in the living room with a newspaper in his hands. He nearly doubled over when he saw me.

"Why didn't I know my wife was alive?" I shouted louder than I had intended to, "You helped keep her from me and I intend to know why!"
Alice came running after me. When she approached she looked from me to Frank. Frank rose like he had just seen a ghost. "Collin," he breathed like he was afraid to trust his own eyes. There was a shake present in his voice, "You'd better sit down."

CHAPTER FIFTEEN

Nothing could prepare me for what Frank was about to say. I couldn't begin to understand why they would keep me in the dark about something as crucial as my wife being alive. Sure, Frank and Alice had tried to inform me in the beginning but after that they never tried again. A man needed to know when his wife was alive. I gritted my teeth and forced myself to sit in a chair opposite from Frank.

Frank pinched his mustache with his index finger and thumb. Last I saw him he didn't even have a mustache. Come to think of it, Alice looked a little older too. She now had a slight case of crow's feet forming near her eyes. Frank watched me for some time, probably wondering what to say. It wasn't every day his ex- son-in-law stormed in to the living room demanding an explanation as to why he didn't know his wife was alive.

Frank shifted in his seat as he began, "We tried, Collin. I realize we didn't try as hard as we should have. I'm sorry. " I grunted. Frank was surprised at my reactions since he'd never seen me angry before. My hands clenched into fists. I had to convince myself to release them. "Once Julia found out for herself that you were in fact, remarried, she told us to never contact you again. She wanted you to move on and forget. She wanted you to be happy."
I shook my head, "Forget? That is impossible,

Frank. I've never been able to forget her, not one day. Julia is my wife. You kept my wife from me. I don't care what she told you," I thrust my index finger in the air to point at him, "You know and I know that you should have told me anyway." I knew I could have lived the rest of my life without ever knowing the truth. The thought of never being able to be with Julia again gutted me. "You would deny me my wife?" Tension clenched in my chest. I was so angry I could hardly see straight.

"I am sorry, Collin. I really am, Alice and I both. We tried to reason with her but she made us promise not to contact you." I knew how stubborn and willful Julia could be. I had no reason not to believe him. So far everything lined up with what Julia had told me. Frank leaned back in his seat, "I'm the villain, I know this, but Collin please hear me out. I can't imagine what you went through or what you are feeling now. If someone had kept my wife from me for four years I would probably want to kill the man," I set my jaw as Frank continued to watch me, "But it wasn't easy for us to watch Julia wither away like she did."

"What are you talking about?" I wanted him to speak plainly to me.

"She cried all the time. You know how she loves to cook," I nodded, "For a year she refused to step foot in the kitchen. She hated cooking. She said it reminded her of when she used to make blueberry pancakes for breakfast on your birthday." I wondered how I could forget something as simple and beautiful as that. My mouth used to water thinking about the pancakes as she made them. Frank continued, "She didn't sleep much. We took her to the doctor so she could get a prescription to help her sleep. Alice encouraged her to delve into her new career. Julia probably told you but she had to leave everything behind. We couldn't have her visit here because people might recognize her and it would disrupt your life so she moved by the bayou. We were so worried about her and sometimes, we still are. What you need to remember is she did it all for you."

It felt like a frog had lodged itself in my throat. I couldn't speak even if I wanted to.

Alice had been standing the entire time, no doubt from nervousness. She waved her hand at me so that I would look at her. Julia still loves you very much, she signed. I can see that you still love her too. But C-O-L-L-I-N, Alice finger spelled my name.

I corrected her with the sign name she had given me when Julia and I were dating.

Alice was surprised I remembered it and repeated the sign. She continued, It is hard for her but she understands. You are married now. You must honor your new wife and God.

"God?" I rose to my feet and shouted, "Why would God let something like this happen?" I paced the floor for a few seconds then vented, "You know what is so sick about all of this mess?"

Frank waited for me to tell him. "Everyone, especially Julia, is so certain that God knows what he is doing! I know I shouldn't say things like that but at this point there really isn't much to stop me. He took my wife away from me then he let her live, oh but only so she wouldn't remember me. I go on thinking she is still dead and marry someone else and no one, not even God himself stops me. I see my wife at the church and have to run after her but she escapes me. My own wife is running from me! When I finally see her again she tells me to not contact her because I won't be able to find her again!"

Frank stuck a hand in the air to stop me. "That's right; she goes by a different name now. You wouldn't be able to find her."

"And I suppose you won't tell me what that name is."

Frank shook his head, "Sorry."

"Let me guess: she made you promise," Frank nodded, "Well isn't that wonderful? I am her husband and I can't be with my own wife. Do you want to know something? I can't even enjoy being at home because my new wife accuses me of thinking of Julia," I paused then asked, "How can God be so cruel?

Frank waited a moment then answered, "I don't pretend to know why God is letting this happen. I can only imagine that this can help strengthen your faith and Julia's as well."

"Have you talked to her today?" I was hoping he had.

"No," Frank shook his head, "I haven't talked to her in about… two days."
"That's when I saw her again."
Frank's eyes grew then he relaxed them, "I know this is probably the worst situation imaginable and I can only imagine how angry you are with Alice and I but I want you to know that I am glad you stopped by. After Julia's supposed death it hasn't been the same without you around."
Alice nodded. She must have been reading Frank's lips the entire time.
"I really did want to tell you about Julia, Collin, but Julia wouldn't conceive of it. She's always been like that, putting others above herself." I nodded and rose from my seat. Frank did the same. "You should go home to your wife. I bet she is worried sick."

Alice embraced me and pointed to a picture frame on the mantle in their living room. I had been there countless times before with Julia and now it seemed so strange to be there without her. The last time I was here we were all family and now we were practically strangers. Now that my anger had begun to subside I noticed the same scent of black cherries as I did when I first met the Douglasses and tried to smile. I looked to where Alice was pointing on the mantle. There was a picture of Frank and Alice with Julia and I on our wedding day. Next to it was another photograph from our wedding but this one was a close up of Julia and I. My heart ached. She looked breathtakingly gorgeous.

I stepped closer and took the frame in my hands. I touched Julia's mouth. A lump formed in my throat and it felt like something seized my chest. That was always how I thought of Julia. Beautiful, breathtaking, radiant and untouchable in her wedding gown she had hand made. I remembered the way she looked when we exchanged vows and that smile of hers that could melt me. I set the frame back in its place on the mantle. I wanted to ask Frank and Alice if I could have a copy of the picture but then recalled that I had stashed them all away once Karen and I married. Besides, they probably wouldn't let me take a copy anyway seeing as how I was remarried now. But seeing those pictures on their mantle floored me. It had been three years since I had been out of the picture. I was no longer a part of their family and yet there was my picture in the most displayed part of their home. I knew Frank and Alice were not able to have any more children aside from Julia. They had told me the story before. Frank had a problem with his sperm count and it was a miracle Julia was ever able to enter the world. Frank placed his hand on my shoulder. I swallowed.

Alice caught my attention and signed, Please forgive us, Collin. We are so sorry. You are still like a son to us and we love you. Don't be angry at God.

I shook my head, completely surprised that

my feelings of bitterness toward them had dissipated. I knew God must have been working on my heart even as I had shouted how angry I was with him. I was amazed at how the couple before me could witness everything I had and was still able to trust God, much less forgive me for remarrying and still think of me as a son.

I held up my right hand and replied to Alice, I love you both too. Alice's eyes widened and she gave me another hug. She thought I had lost my touch with ASL when really I had lost touch with everyone and everything, especially God.

CHAPTER SIXTEEN

I entered my house through the front door. I couldn't hear any noise. Normally the T.V. or the radio could be heard from where I was but today there was no noise to be heard. That was a bad sign. I didn't know what to expect. I had no idea how to tell Karen what happened and for the first time since the events started to unravel I wondered whether or not Karen would believe me when I said I did not have sex with Julia. It would be hard for her to believe me, I thought as I wondered how I would feel if I were in her shoes. If roles were reversed I would probably want to find Karen's ex-husband and punch his lights out. I had never called her to let her know I was safe or that I would be home a day later. I wondered what she went through when Alvin told her that I was with Julia and that he had seen her with his own eyes.

I paced myself as I walked further through the house looking for Karen. She wasn't downstairs. I made my way up the stairs and entered our bedroom. There she was sprawled out on the bed with a package of Kleenexes and soiled tissues strewn out next to her. The television wasn't on in our bedroom either. When I entered the room she didn't even look at me. Instead she continued to focus on the white wall opposite our bed. I leaned on the edge of our bed and watched Karen's body tilt as I steadied myself on the bed to kick off my shoes. I slid off my shirt and tossed it on the end of the bed. I stood there for a moment watching her. She had yet to blink. I walked toward her and took sat by her. I moved the soiled Kleenexes from the bed and pushed them away from me so I could sit down further.

"I'm sorry, Karen," the words rushed out of my mouth, "I should have called you. It was selfish and inconsiderate of me. And…"
Karen cut me off, "She's alive, isn't she?"
"Yes."
Karen lifted her eyes to look at me. They were cold and impersonal. "What was it like to see her again?"
Her question took me off guard. There had to be a catch in it somewhere. My mind fuddled as I began to answer her. I furrowed my brow, "It was… like seeing a ghost."
"A very pretty ghost." I said nothing. She began to open her mouth again. I stopped her.
"I didn't have sex with her, Karen. I know that is what you are going to ask me. I didn't," I studied Karen as she nodded. "I'm married to you," I said it partly for Karen and partly because I needed to hear it myself.
"But you love her," Karen's words felt like they were a ton of bricks that suddenly slammed into me, "don't you?"

I wanted to say something, though I didn't have the right words to say. I knew she wanted me to tell her that I didn't love Julia anymore. That perhaps we were two different people now who had grown a world apart and were now strangers. That my love for Karen had overcome my love for Julia and I thought only of Karen. But I couldn't. The truth was harsh. Instead of reassuring Karen with a lie, I remained silent, debating what exactly I could say to make her feel better without actually lying. But nothing came to me. I didn't like seeing her like this.

"Right," Karen nodded again. Tears began to form in her eyes. I pulled the last tissue from the Kleenex box and handed it to her. I felt uneasy as I rushed to the bathroom to roll up some toilet paper in my hand. I could hear Karen mumble something from the bedroom to the effect of "Of course you do. And of course she is resurrected from the dead."

I decided to let it go. When I reached for the toilet paper I saw an EPT lying on top of the counter. I knew what it meant. I had read too many manuals on EPT when Karen thought she could be pregnant the first time around. I was no rookie when it came to them. I tried to gather my senses as I bunched the pieces of toilet paper in my hand and retraced my steps to the bedroom. I handed Karen the tissues. She began to cry even more. I sucked in my breath.

"I suppose you know," She spoke through

gasping sobs for breath, "that I'm pregnant."

The air rushed out of my body and my knees felt weak. I wondered if I had heard her correctly but I knew I had because I'd seen the EPT result for myself. I also knew exactly when Karen had conceived.

She couldn't be more than a month along. It was the night I'd come home from the church dazed and confused about what I'd seen. Julia was all over my mind and I couldn't suppress the idea that it was her I had seen fleeing the church and not looking back as I chased her.

I had been so exhausted that night but Karen had sought assurance that I still loved her, especially after the fight we'd had in the kitchen before I left. I had felt guilty for the things I said to Karen. I had felt even guiltier for thinking about Julia as I lay in bed next to my wife. After I pushed Karen's advances away the first time, I'd reached out for her when she turned her back to me.

Looking back I think I did it partly to prove to Karen that I did still care for her and partly because I wanted to assure myself that I hadn't seen Julia that night. Because if I had I would have lived three… four years without her when she had been under my nose the entire time. But as it so happened that was exactly the way things were.

And now Karen was definitely pregnant this time. I was going to be a father.

CHAPTER SEVENTEEN

Months passed by and Karen's stomach began to swell. It looked like she had a medium sized balloon hidden beneath her shirt. Karen would wake me up in the middle of the night as her cravings hit her. She started to complain about the ache in her lower back and asked me to get some food for her.

Crackers with peanut butter and green olives were her staples. In the event that I wouldn't hear her requests for food she would heave a heavy sigh and waddle her way downstairs. I would inevitably wake up a few minutes later to find her just reaching the bottom of the stairs. Karen would put her hands on her hips when she saw me and smile. She'd then shake her head and continue to waddle toward the kitchen. She often sweated throughout the day and I'd have to force her to stop cleaning the house and make her sit down. When I couldn't find her she normally had her head leaning over the toilet bowl as she puked.

A week after Karen told me she was pregnant she rushed to the nearest bookstore and picked out a copy of the most unique baby names of the year. She said she wanted a baby name that would reflect who the baby would be. When she talked like that I tended to drown in visions of a baby popping out of Karen with hair like Einstein's.

But more often than I'd like I thought of Julia. I had just thought there was no way we could be together before. But now I was entirely certain. Not only was I married to someone else, but Julia went by a different name now. She didn't want me to find her again and Karen was pregnant with our child. It seemed wrong to me on so many levels. Julia had told me many times before how she longed to be a mother one day and give me everything she could. She'd wanted a little person made up of the both of us. But she couldn't have children. And that was before I thought she was dead. That was before I'd remarried and found out Julia was actually alive. That was before Karen conceived our child.

Julia was out there somewhere living her life without me. She was never one to complain much but I could imagine how she felt. I wondered where she was and what she was doing. I wondered if she had moved on to a new job as a nurse at another school to allow me to have the chance to be "happy." My mind ventured to the possibility that she was dating someone. The very idea of it made me angry. I winced when I thought of it. It was difficult for me to imagine someone ever being as close to Julia as I once was… to be able to date her, see her, not have to hide my love for her from anyone. Someone else could smell her perfume she always dabbed on her neck and behind her ears. Someone else could now enjoy the intimacy of being with her. She was free to remarry… to remarry someone else that wasn't me. Julia could adopt a family and have the life she had dreamt of living with me… The life we dreamt living together but weren't given the chance to have. But what got me worse than anything else was not being able to talk to her. Oh how I missed the sound of her voice. Just hearing it had a way of calming me down. And her laugh, God, I missed her laugh. She was alive but I couldn't talk to her. It hurt like hell. There wasn't a damn thing I could do about it.

She'd never said she would wait on for me in a one in a billion chance that we would be reunited in the future should Karen pass away before me and neither Julia or I died before we had the chance to actually reunite. And why would she? She had no reason to. I thought about Julia a lot, much more than I would ever admit, especially when I pushed paper work at the lawyer's office. It reminded me of the wide turn I took to get where I was. I thought of my grandfather and contemplated how he felt, if it was anything similar to the way I did.

It was now October and the leaves were exchanging their lazy green for rich browns, golden yellows and ruby reds. It was one of those days that I was missing her badly. Don't get me wrong, every day was hard without Julia but on days like this it hurt to breathe. Her memory filled the air. And true to tradition, when the breeze blew in so did Julia just like the first day we met. Just like on our wedding day. Just like when I saw her again on the bayou.

I swallowed hard. I knew exactly what today was. I'd known the day had been coming for months and couldn't erase the date even if I tried. It was October fifth… Julia's birthday. And it seemed wrong to not be there celebrating it with her. She was twenty-eight today. I suddenly felt we were terribly old and held the nagging feeling that we were wasting what precious time we had left on earth living without each other. I thought for maybe the hundredth time about the picture of us that was sitting on Julia's nightstand. I wondered if it was still there and hoped it was. She deserved more than that picture. I knew the tangible items from our marriage were lost. She probably had no other pictures. But I did. I wanted to give them to her to let her know I was still with her. But I didn't even know where she was.

I ran a packet of photographs back and forth against my hand as I stared out the window in my office. I'd gone through my stash of photographs earlier. I'd pretty much decided to drive by Julia's place, or at least the cabin she'd lived in months ago, and deliver the pictures to her. That is, if she even still lived there. The buzzard on my call waiting kept going off and I kept ignoring it. As far as I was concerned I was already gone. I needed to prepare what I would say to her if she would let me.

As I drove down a long stretch of road from the office toward Julia's cabin, I loosened my tie. It felt like it was choking me and I couldn't breathe. My palms grew sweaty and I licked my lips more than once. The air felt stuffy in the car and rightfully so because I paused my deep concentration on what I'd say to Julia, to look out the window. Storm clouds were rolling in from the south. Of course, rain. Drops began to dance on my car's windshield. They grew stronger and heavier until I thought they might pound the windshield out of its place. The rain was so thick I could hardly see to turn onto the narrow gravel road that led to Julia's cabin. I eased my vehicle into her driveway and waited. For what I don't know. I suppose I was waiting for a sign.

My heart beat crazily. I hated coming back here like this. In truth I did it every day. When I wasn't here I wished I were. And that is why I hated being here because I felt like a traitor. I didn't understand why we couldn't just love each other and it be okay. I wanted an answer for why we couldn't be together.

I grabbed the packet of pictures from the passenger seat and waited a few seconds. Her black car was in the driveway. She was actually home, at least for the moment. My heart skipped a beat when I saw her pass by the curtain in the front of the cabin. It looked like she was wearing a blue top and maybe some blue jeans. As I exited the vehicle and approached her door I thought of all the things I wanted to say, planned to say. Like, there is not a day that goes by that I do not think of you or find you in some place. You are a part of me, the part that never dies. You grow stronger each day and I can never bring myself to put you down. I think of you all the time--- every minute

of every day. And I wish that things were easier and could be the way we feel they ought to be. I wish I didn't have to leave you. I miss hearing your voice, seeing your smile. I miss you. So much. I wouldn't trade what we had for the world. If she ever went to heaven before me, she would be the first person I would look for and the only soul I would want to see.
My knees grew weak. I could feel them trying to buckle under. My hands shook terribly. If I didn't know any better I would think my bones were rattling. Rain fell on me hard. I was beginning to think I resembled a drowned rat standing there near the bayou. I knew she couldn't see me. I knew she didn't realize I was here. But then a light came on at the front of the cabin from inside. I watched Julia's body draw toward the window.

Curtains separated her view from me but I began to wonder if she felt my presence or maybe she simply knew I was there. A light shone through the curtains around her blonde hair that made her look like an angel with a halo. Words caught in my throat. My hands shook even more so and I fought hard not to fall apart. So many times I had imagined a moment much like this one. A moment where we were near each other. But it seemed there was always something separating us. I lived in a world that didn't exist anymore, a world of make believe. I wondered if maybe Julia lived in it too. I thought of her wedding band I gave to her the day we married and how right it looked resting on her slender finger. If I didn't do this now I never would.

I quickly placed the packet on her doormat out of the pathway of the rain. I stole one last look at her shadow. "Happy birthday, Julia," I whispered knowing she couldn't hear me. I wished I could spend it with her and give her everything she ever wanted. But I couldn't. I knew my place. I had to leave. I took a few steps from the door when I heard it swing open.

I froze, I mean really froze. I could hear her breathing. I knew she saw me now. The rain grew even fiercer and I thought myself stupid for thinking she couldn't see me standing out here. Had she been wondering what I was doing in her yard all along?

She said nothing. She would let me leave.

I remembered something that would mean more to her on her birthday than anything else. It was my most prized possession and I never went without it. I don't know how I mustered the courage to turn and face her but I did.

She was radiant, absolutely radiant. Julia was in fact wearing a blue top and jeans. She stood there studying me. I knew she was taking me in as much as I was taking in her. A wisp of blonde hair fell in her face. I could see tears beginning to form in her eyes but she held them back. Her peach complexion looked just as smooth as ever. Something about her gave a huge tug at my heart. I pulled my wedding band, the one she gave me on our wedding day, from my pants pocket. I walked slowly toward her. Julia extended her hand. Her eyes questioned me as I released my fist and placed the wedding band in the palm of her hand. She stared at it for a second and swallowed hard. I thought she might say something, but she didn't. I had hoped to say something but couldn't. All I could do was look at her. Julia lifted her eyes from the wedding band to me. She held them there. I stood there a second more then nodded and backed away. I was out from under the awning and susceptible to the weather now.

Julia jumped a step as if considering whether or not to go after me. She relented. I continued to strive for my car. It was very difficult to turn away from her. I had toyed with the idea of what I would say to her if given the chance but it wasn't right. I was convicted of that now.

I shouldn't be here. I shouldn't still love her.

I said nothing to Julia. Julia said nothing to me. I saw her bend down to pick up the packet of pictures. Her other hand was holding on tightly to my wedding band. I climbed in my vehicle, met her eyes as I closed the door, and drove away.

I couldn't think of much on the way home except I had broken the tenth commandment: Thou shalt not covet thy neighbor's wife. Okay, so Julia wasn't my wife anymore but I was married. And she was off limits. And even if I wasn't going against number ten I was going against the adultery one.

As I entered the house Karen came scurrying

from the living room, "What happened to you?" She asked bewildered, at seeing me soaking wet. She left to go get a towel to help dry me off. "Rain," I said.

Chapter Eighteen

Then one afternoon nearly six months after the news of Karen's pregnancy, I came home from work in an exceptionally good mood.

When Karen asked why I was so happy I told her, "I quit the office."
"You what?" She asked.
"I'm going back to the lumber yard. I talked to the owner today and he told me I could go back with twice the hourly wages I originally had. Told me he remembered what a hard worker I was. He said he could use my legal knowledge to help him come up with some solutions for the industry...." I rattled on as I slapped my hands on the counter top. For the first time since Julia's death I was actually looking forward to going to work. Karen was silent until I finished.
"How do you plan to support me and the baby? I can't work in my last term."
"I just told you. They bumped up my hourly wage twice what it originally was."
"Even so, there is no way you can support all of us. It's not just you and me. Now there is a baby on the way. You need an adult job for an adult life." My right eye twitched when she said it. I tried to keep my disappointment that was now coupled with agitation under wraps. "What is it?" Karen asked.
"When you asked me to drop what I loved doing

for what you thought was acceptable, I did it. I didn't try to make you feel bad about it. I just did what you asked. I've been doing what you wanted for our life for over three years now and well Karen, I know this is the worst time to tell you when you are pregnant but I had imagined that you could at least pretend to be happy that I am happy."

"This is not about you! You think everything is about you, Collin! This is about the baby!"

I took a step back and weighed the words that would spill from my mouth next. "So, has your entire aim been to have a baby with me? Is that what this was all about? You just want a baby. You don't care who you have to have it with or who you have to ask out on a date. You want the dream life but you don't care who it is with or what it costs them. And you know very well I could support us on the income from the lumber yard."

Karen grew angry then. "Oh, you have some nerve!" She turned on her swollen feet and then turned around just as quickly. "Is this about her again?" I waited.

"Her who, Karen?" My tone dared her to say the name.

Her face grew flush with anger, "You know who I am talking about!"

I leaned forward, "Julia?"

She looked like she would explode. "First you don't even want to mention her name and now you are dying to say it?"

"You know what? I love you even though you may not believe me. But I can't pretend like you aren't using this baby to trap me. You are so afraid of me leaving you that you have to use an innocent child to get what you want." Karen's eyes flickered with intensity. "You know it's true. I haven't left you because I'm married to you." "But you're also married to her," Karen placed a hand on her right hip and gritted her teeth. "This is who I am. Don't try to change me," I watched her expression. Karen hadn't even tried to contradict my theory on her trapping me with the baby. "Look, I'm sorry this is how things turned out with us. Please forgive me. I wanted more for us." I stepped out of the room and went upstairs.

I changed into some sweats and headed for the front door. I told Karen I was going for a jog and would be back shortly. She'd said nothing. I thought she was still angry.

My shoes hit the pavement with a fierce intensity as I ran. I hadn't a clue how Karen and I could work out everything. Instead of feeling better as I ran, I felt the same. So I began to pray. I hated the person I had become and I couldn't stand to remain in the life I resided in. I gave up on jogging and returned home. I had only been a few streets over from the house but when I jogged toward the front steps, I noticed Karen's car was gone. Where could she be?

CHAPTER NINETEEN

JULIA

I couldn't forget him. I peered out the cabin window and looked at the night sky. It felt like just yesterday Collin had turned up at my front door standing there in the rain. I had imagined him in my mind so many times and of all days there he stood on my birthday. I couldn't have wished for a better birthday present. There had been so much bubbling up from inside me that when I saw him I thought he could read me and the great vulnerability I felt. I wanted to tell him to stay. I wanted to tell him not to leave. I wanted to believe we could be together again. I still want to believe that.

Collin was just as handsome as the last time I had seen him. He'd always been that way to me. The first time I met him, his chestnut hair and dark eyes reminded me of a Louisiana swamp. Call me strange, but as a little girl I enjoyed venturing off to those places. I grew up near the bayou so looking into Collin's eyes had instantly become home to me. And when I saw him on my birthday, it was like I was finally home again… with him. If it hadn't been for those horribly nagging reminders in my mind that he was now married… to someone else, I would have run to him and pressed my lips to his. I had wanted to do the same thing when I saw him on the bayou. Only

God knows how terribly difficult it was for me to restrain myself from him. Collin smelt the way he always had, like a mixture between the deep woods and mint. He even looked better than I remembered. Sometimes if I closed my eyes I could imagine him beside me. He would be laughing at a joke or making those bug eyes he normally did when something I said caught him off guard. As far as I was concerned, Collin was lounging on the sofa, fixing me sweet tea, or standing next to me breathing in the scent of my hair. He used to do things like that and now those were all things I missed. I missed him horribly. And yet he was everywhere.

    I pushed a few strands of hair behind my ear and decided to light a fire in the fire place. Since I'd already had Mike chop the wood for me, all I had to do was light the fire. I thought of the last time I'd actually lit one. It was with Collin. The memory pierced my mind. I could still feel his arms around me and I could still envision the look in his eyes as he wiped my tears. He was my husband. Tears fought their way to my eyes but I managed to hold them off… for now. As I lit the firewood thoughts flooded my mind. Horrible thoughts that led me to wonder if he was making love to his wife now. My entire being shuddered. The thought was repulsive. It had been four years since we'd made love and I had my doubts that he remembered any of it. I never got a goodbye. I wasn't given the chance of a goodbye kiss. The last night we made love had been a night much like this one. It was suddenly cold outside and a fierce wind sang. Collin had watched me make some chili in the kitchen and out of nowhere swept me up into his arms and laughed as he carried me to our bedroom. It had been dark in our bedroom but the moonlight was bright enough that I could see him if I moved right. He kept calling my name, Julia… It was the night I had conceived. My heart ached.

I rose from the fire place and shook my head. I wrapped my sweater tighter around me. Things were different now. They could never go back to the way things were. I still loved him. But it was no use now. He was married and I? Well, I was engaged. My hands ran over my abdomen.

It had been so traumatic for me when I came out of the coma. I didn't believe my parents when they told me I was pregnant. I knew I was married and I knew Collin's name but I couldn't remember what he looked like. I didn't remember that I was pregnant and I certainly could not fathom why he was not there until Mom told me the truth. My memories of mine and Collin's life together came later. Once she told me Collin remarried, I refused to eat. I was dying inside.

Then one night, I had stolen Dad's car since I didn't have a driver's license anymore, and drove to my tombstone. I had pulled a wooden bat from Dad's back seat that he always kept for batting practice when he coaches the little league. I had tightened my wrists so tight around the bat that they began to turn blue. I swung at my tombstone with all my might. But no matter how hard I swung I couldn't tear it down. Pieces of wood were strewn around the tombstone. I remember pausing only long enough to sigh and strike the tombstone with a kick. I kicked it until I thought I couldn't kick it anymore. When all my energy was finally spent I sat on my empty grave and waited. I was waiting for Collin to come back to me. I thought he would show at some point. But he didn't. Excruciating cramps seized my stomach. I wanted to scream it hurt so bad. I ended up lying in a ball on the dewy grass holding my abdomen. Mom and Dad eventually showed up after the pains ceased. They weren't even angry. They tried to get me to talk but all I said was "The baby."

I couldn't go to the hospital so they sent for the doctor to meet us at the house. And he did. He examined me until I was sick of seeing his face. I think he kept hoping he would hear the baby's heartbeat. But he didn't. I had lost Collin and our baby. And Collin never knew that we would have had a son.

But that was the past now. It had to be. Mike was a good man, solid and strong. He was the principal of the new school I worked at and he loved children. We had been nothing but friends until after I had seen Collin again. Mike had a way of making children mind without having to play the role of the enemy. And for a reason that made me uncomfortable. I was thankful he was away at a school board conference. I wouldn't want him to see me like this and certainly not over Collin. I suppose it was the loneliness of being without Collin that drove me to Mike. Mike didn't know much of the story by any means, but he knew enough for me. He knew I had an ex-husband. He also knew that I had to turn my life upside down after it ended. But that's the problem, isn't it? My own conscience was convicting me now. It never ended between you and Collin. It still hasn't ended.

I sat on the sofa now and closed my eyes. It was nights like this that I felt the loneliest. God, I realize things are complicated but I want to see Collin again. I know I told him to leave me alone and to never look for me again but that was because I was scared. I was afraid of what I might do if I saw him again. I just want him in my life. I want my husband back. Why is that so wrong? Tears streamed down my face. I lay down on the sofa and watched the flames flicker near my face. I pulled the chain from my neck out of my sweater. I stared at Collin's wedding band on it and toyed with it in my hands for a moment. I know you still love me, Collin. I love you too. I propped my elbow on the sofa and leaned my head in my left hand. My heart had performed a million summersaults when I saw that Collin kept his wedding band I had given him. I knew why he gave it to me. It was his way of telling me his heart or at least part of it was still with me. He didn't want me to feel alone. But still, a nasty thought captured hold of my mind taunting me with the thought that he'd given me his wedding band as a way to say it was finally over between us and he didn't need it anymore. I fiddled with his band and ran a finger over the inside of it where an engraving read *Forever.*

I heard a tap. Then another tap. My head shot up. Am I imagining it or--- Just then I heard it again. It was coming closer to where I sat. My heart began to pound.

I whipped my head around to see where exactly it was coming from and that's when I saw her. The same woman I saw with Collin years ago. Her long dark hair hung in her face. It looked wild to me. So did her eyes. There was a hate present in them and once I saw it, it made me want to jump back. I hadn't a clue what she was here for. She stepped toward me slowly.

I flinched. "Why are you here?" She said nothing. I tried again, the words unwilling to pour from my tongue, "How did you get in?" I began to stand but she shoved me back on the sofa.

"Why?" She asked, without regard to my own questions.

"Excuse me?" I hadn't a clue what she was talking about.

Her voice grew louder with rage, "Why was it not enough for you?" She waited a second then pulled a gun out of her pants pocket. "Let me guess, you're Julia." I had tried so hard to forget her name, to forget this woman's face. She was just a reminder of the pain from separation that was ever present with me. But no matter how I tried, I could not wipe her name from my mind. It taunted me. Her name was Karen. It constantly filled my mind.

I nodded. "Yes, but I don't know what you are talking about." I tried my best not to be afraid but I couldn't help it. She was some crazy woman that broke into my cabin. And I could only ascertain that she knew Collin still loved me.

"My husband!" She shut her eyes and screamed the words, "I do everything and still you are all he sees." So maybe she assumed I still loved him and if she did, her assumption was correct which only made me more concerned. I began to fumble behind me for my cell phone I had sat on the couch earlier.

"How did you find me?"

"That was easy," She said with a flippant voice, "I followed him. I had to see if he would go back to you. And he always does. You know what I don't get is what is it about you that makes you so irreplaceable to him? You'd think you were Aphrodite or something," She waved the gun around.

"What's---"

She narrowed her eyes at me. "He probably didn't tell you my name did he? It's Karen." I didn't want to respond to that one. "Do you know I'm pregnant? With his baby? But all he wants is you!" Karen lunged at me and grabbed me by the hair. She forced me to stand. I didn't want to hurt her. I knew she must be in enough pain as it was. But when she said she was pregnant I couldn't help but think she was telling the truth. Her baby was

Collin's. Her stomach was unmistakably huge. It felt like my heart was crumbling inside of me. I didn't want to believe her. Karen shoved the gun under my chin and pressed it hard to me. The barrel was cold.
"Forgive me," I whispered before I could think about it.
"What?" Karen hissed.
"Please, forgive me," Karen was listening now, "It's not your fault. You got caught up in this and I am sorry. I never meant to hurt you. He never meant to hurt you. I know he didn't."
"But he did. You did," Karen jerked harder at my hair. "The morning he came home after he spent the evening with you he didn't so much as want to look at me. Have you any idea what that is like?!" She shrieked. I could hear the pain in her voice but soon even that turned sinister. "But he made love to me that night," She whispered in my ear. I tried to jerk away but she pulled even harder to make certain I would hear the next part, "And he enjoyed it." I was sick now. Horribly sick.

I'd had enough. She'd hurt me in the worst way imaginable. I shoved her back and when she came running for me, I swung in a punch that hit her jaw so hard I heard my knuckles clash with it. I watched Karen fall back She didn't stay back for long. Karen charged forward and shot the gun past my right ear. I screamed bloody murder. Just then I heard a pound come from my front door. Then a crash. I ducked down on the floor and covered my face with my hands. The first thing that came to mind was it was another bullet shooting toward me. I thought of the shooting at the convenience store. I thought of my plan to tell Collin about the baby the night I had gone for the milk to make us some dinner. I thought of all those things. *God, help!*

A gun shot pierced the air. I jumped and my entire body shook. I began to breathe hard then realized I didn't feel any pain in my body. The shot didn't hit me. I uncovered my head and looked toward Karen. She was lying on the floor with blood gushing from her chest. Police ran past me and hovered over her body.

Several policemen made their way toward me and asked "Are you alright miss?" I shook my head, unable to speak. "Yes," The tallest policeman said as if he could read my mind, "She's dead. What happened here miss? A man on the lake heard the commotion and sent us out." My mind was racing so fast I could hardly comprehend what he was saying.

CHAPTER TWENTY

COLLIN

I kept driving around, trying to figure out where Karen could be. Maybe she had finally left me.

It was dark outside and much too cold for Karen to be out for a walk. She wasn't much of a night owl anyway. A thought held me captive. What if... Just what if Karen has found Julia? My heart raced. Even if it was nothing, even if it was just a silly notion of fear, I had to investigate it. I rationalized that I would just drive by Julia's cabin and make sure she was okay. I wouldn't have to go in or talk to her, just make certain she was in no danger.

I turned onto the narrow gravel road leading to Julia's cabin.

My cell phone sounded. "Collin, its Phil."

Phil was the sheriff of the police department. I had put in a call to him nearly two hours ago when I first realized Karen was missing. Karen was missing and she didn't want to be found. I didn't know what else to do at the time except call Phil. I knew after I called the police they would be laughing: Collin has lost his pregnant wife. I knew jokes like that would ensue.

"Collin, you'd better get down to this cabin,"

there was something hidden deep in Phil's voice, "We've found---"

I didn't bother listening to the rest of it. I knew then that Karen was at Julia's. I knew something had happened. I could only pray that I wasn't too late.

I pressed my foot hard on the gas pedal and raced to Julia's cabin, kicking up a dirt cloud behind me the entire way. Those seconds seemed like an eternity. Nothing could get me to Julia's cabin fast enough.

When I arrived, I heard nothing as I walked inside. Oh, I knew there was noise, there had to be. Policemen were taping off Julia's cabin in yellow caution tape. They were carrying things in and out of the cabin. People were opening and closing their mouths but I heard none of it. My heart slammed in my chest. Julia or Karen or maybe even both of them was gone. It was all my fault. I shoved my way through the police and emergency medical technicians. Phil saw me and tried to keep me steady with his aged hands. "Now Collin, just take a minute…" He said, "Take a minute then go on in." I didn't want to listen to any of it. He'd never been in my situation. I prayed as I pushed him out of the way and forged inside Julia's cabin.

It was dark inside with only a small lamp illuminating a corner of the living room. There was a fire dwindling in the fire place. It had to be crackling, but I didn't notice it. I was too busy looking for Julia and Karen. What if something happened to the baby? Chalk outlined the form of a body on the right side of Julia's living room. My stomach clenched. If it was Julia or Karen, I had no idea. My hands began to tremble. And that was when I saw her.

Julia was curled up in a tiny ball beneath the window in the living room. She looked depleted of any strength she once had. She hastily rocked back and forth. Tears streamed down her face. The first thing I thought was, she's hurt. I opened my mouth to speak but nothing came out. I edged toward her. Julia fixated her eyes on my shoes, and then noticing it was me, lifted her eyes slowly to meet mine. She was moving her lips so I figured she had to be whispering something. I sat on the floor next to her and grabbed her hand. It was just as small and fragile as I had remembered it to be. I wanted to take her in my arms and hold her, to tell her that whatever happened would be alright. She was shaking. Julia heaved a heavy sigh that sounded like the weight of the world unfolding and leaned her head on my shoulder. She wrapped her arms around me, which took me off guard. Through heavy sighs I heard her say, "Sorry. I'm so… sorry…" I took my index finger and lifted her chin with it. I searched her eyes for the answer to my question. And there the answer was, written all over her face.

Julia looked past me. I craned my head to look behind me. There was an EMT with a stretcher rolling Karen out of the cabin. Blood was covering the top of her shirt. Her eyes were closed and she looked strangely pale. Someone had placed an air mask over her nose and mouth for oxygen. Tubes were hooked up to the gurney. It felt like an invisible hand was clasped around my throat.

"My God," I breathed, "What happened?"
The EMT, obviously new at his job replied with, "I'm sorry, sir. We're taking her to St. Joseph Hospital." With that he wheeled her out of the cabin and loaded her into the back of the ambulance.
I thought things were as terrible as they could get. But I was wrong, so very wrong. Julia tugged at my hand. When I turned toward her, she squeezed it. "Go be with your wife, Collin. She needs you." I was torn in two opposing directions. The words that had been tangled on my tongue since I arrived finally made their way to the surface, "Are you okay? Julia, what happened to you?" I reached my hand out to cradle her face. Whatever Karen had done went terribly wrong and it had shaken Julia's soul up. "Just tell me you'll be fine and I'll go." I hated what Karen had done to her. The only thing I possibly hated more was myself for not getting there in time to prevent it.

A tall man with irritatingly perfect features rushed up to Julia and wrapped her in his arms. Who the hell was he? Julia let him hold her. She peeked her heavenly eyes over his shoulder to look at me. Air was rushing out of my body. I felt like I'd been knocked back in a boxing ring, something I'd experienced in high school only this was a thousand times worse. I wasn't losing a boxing match, I was losing Julia. I had to remind myself to breathe.

"My God, I'm glad you're okay! You have no idea how worried I was when I heard…" He quickly kissed her on the mouth. I clenched my fists so tight that I couldn't feel my hands anymore. I wanted to hurt him so bad. "Julia," The man I wanted to hit with everything in me said, "Who is this man?" He pulled away from her for a moment.
Julia said nothing. And really, what could she say: this is my husband?
I waited for her to say something but she didn't. "No one," I answered for her. I turned to leave as quickly as my feet would carry me. If I didn't hurry, the ambulance would leave without me.

CHAPTER TWENTY-ONE

Everything passed by in a whirl. Faces became blurs, noises became echoes. Siren lights were not only horrifying, they were also annoying. I was sitting at Karen's bedside at the hospital with my head in my hands. I couldn't look at her. I knew I should feel compassion for her; she was after all, my wife. I did marry her out of love. I swore to take care of her. We'd conceived a child together that was growing inside her womb. And yet all these things were not enough. Not anymore.

She had tried to kill Julia.

The police had already given me the whole spill. Karen, enraged, sought out Julia for revenge. Julia tried to protect herself. A man by the lake overheard Karen breaking into the cabin and had called the police. The police shot Karen when they saw she was going to kill Julia. I knew the brutal facts even if I no longer wanted to. If Karen made it out of here alive, she would face life in prison for attempted murder.

Now it was real. Soon everyone would know that Julia wasn't dead and that she was in fact, still alive. They would know that Karen nearly succeeded in murdering her. They would know something was going on between Julia and I while I was married to Karen, though Julia and I never did anything about it. I was the common factor in all of this. As far as I was concerned, I was the villain. I had turned Karen into a monster. It wasn't Karen who had suddenly decided to become this way. It was me. I made her feel like she wasn't good enough. But Karen was at fault for how she chose the react to it all. Karen was the one who drove to Julia's. Karen was the one who entertained the thought of killing Julia. And it was Karen who held her finger on the trigger, ready to murder Julia. I didn't want to think what would have happened if the police hadn't shown when they did. Julia would be the one lying in the hospital now, not Karen.

Julia could have died. Anger did not even begin to describe what stirred inside of me. I lifted my head from my hands and looked toward Karen. My eyes were starting to refocus from blurs to clarity. Did God really want everyone to remain miserable? Did I have to pay for my mistake every day for the rest of my life? And most importantly, how could I stay married to someone who nearly succeeded in murdering my Julia?

Before I could even attempt to make sense of it all, Karen's doctor walked into the room, the very same room, I might add, that Julia was once in when she was in a coma. I couldn't stand the smell of these sterile rooms. As far as I was concerned, it was a cruel way to help people in a sort of sterile prison. People were locked away from everything and everyone they loved. I tried my best not to take in the room that held so many painful memories for me.

"Mr. Flannigan," A balding doctor extended his hand and shook mine, "I'm afraid that I have some very bad news. Your wife's condition is… Well, it is not its best. She might not make it through the night. She's bleeding internally and the blood is filling her chest." I waited for him to continue. There was more. There was always more. At seeing I was okay, he continued, "We are extracting as much blood as we can but she is bleeding faster than we can extract. And with every extraction, she needs a transfusion. I see she is type O Negative, is that right?" The doctor stole a look at the chart in his hand then looked up at me.

"Yes," I managed.

"That is a bit of a problem. There are not many O Negative donors simply because there are not that many O Negative blood types around here. I've put in a call to the Blood Center. They don't have anything. I am waiting to hear from some more options but it is not looking good. If you know of any O Negative carriers, you should get them here now." Right. Of course I knew everyone's blood type. Of course it would be a synch to find an O Negative. I exhaled slowly. "The baby isn't taking well to the trauma, either. Its heart rate is jumping all over the place. It's like it is going into shock. I'm sorry, but there is not much we can do there either.

"The baby is too young to forcefully remove from your wife's womb. If we did, your wife would die. The best thing we can do for the baby is wait and let it try to come out of the shock on its own," He studied my face then said, "I'll be back in an hour."

I waited for over an hour and still there was no sign of the doctor. I hadn't called Dad or Karen's parents. I didn't want them here. Karen wouldn't want them to see her like this anyway. I began to wonder what was taking so long. I didn't know how to pray any more. It seemed like all possible words and even thoughts had eluded my brain and all that was left had become total mush. I soon realized why the doctor was taking so long when he walked in with Julia.
Julia.
I nearly fell out of my chair but forced legs full of JELLO to stand. She was here. I didn't know what to do. Karen's monitor sounded every few seconds.

"Mr. Flannigan," the doctor began.
"What are you doing here?" I questioned Julia. Her eyes were like doves.
"I'm here to help."
"Help?" She couldn't possibly help me. No one could. She studied me. "You don't need to be here, Julia. Just go home." I answered with more of a snap than I had originally intended. I had to make her leave.
"I can't go home. My cabin is a crime scene," She answered softly.
"Now Mr. Flannigan…" the doctor input, "I

realize this is a trying situation, but Julia can help…"

The words flew from my mouth. "Trying situation? You haven't the slightest. I appreciate everything you've done to try to help us but Julia cannot. And my name is Collin."

"Collin," the doctor tried again, "Julia is O Negative. She'd like to donate blood."

I had tried to zone him out but there was no mistaking what he just said. "No," I replied without a thought.

The doctor seemed baffled at my response. "Absolutely not."

"You don't get a choice in this, Collin. I'm going to help. Now let me help." Julia spoke sternly. She still had splatters of blood on her shirt from Karen, no doubt.

I rested a hand on the doctor's shoulder and walked him toward the door. "Doctor, give us a moment," I said as I shoved him out of the room and took Julia by the arm.

Julia broke free from my hold. She wasted no time in speaking. "The last time I was in here I thought I would die. It feels like forever," Julia spoke while surveying the room, careful not to look at Karen lying on the bed. "I know you must have gone through a lot when you thought I was dead. I don't want you to lose another wife, Collin. I'm not leaving until I donate the blood."

"No!"

"Why?"

"Because I already lost you once and I'm not going

to lose you again." Surprise registered on Julia's face. Words flew out of my mouth before I could arrest them, "Who was that man?" I had to know. Julia gritted her teeth and looked off to the side then met my gaze again. "He's my fiancé."

I took a step back. It felt like the floor had slipped out from under me. Did I hear her correctly? Surely I heard right. My gut clenched. My chest tightened. My heart fell. Air was escaping my body. It felt like someone had just gutted me with a knife and turned it inside fifty times over. I'd heard a guy at work once talk about his run in with a gang member who had done exactly that to him. The doctors had told him it was a miracle he was alive. As far as I was concerned, I wasn't a live. I could say nothing. I just stared at her. I knew my eyes were as wide as saucers and that I looked exactly as I felt but I couldn't help it. She was getting married. My Julia was getting married… to someone else.

"Collin, please…" Julia took a step toward me and tried to grab my hand. I jerked it away and remained where I was.
"When?" was all I could ask.
"Months after you left my cabin. When you came by on my birthday, we were already together."
"You can't do this," I whispered.
Julia looked down at the floor, "You already have."
"And she's dying in this hospital bed!" I motioned

to Karen and continued. "Don't even pretend that it is the same thing. I thought you were dead! No one had ever told me any different and only years later do you resurface that I finally know the truth! But you're going to marry him knowing that I'm alive?"

"And married to another woman!" Julia rose her voice to match mine then halted. When she opened her mouth to speak again, her voice was soft. "His name is Mike."

"I don't care what the hell his name is!" I shot back.

"Don't even try to turn this around on me. I am coping with this the best way I know how," Julia grabbed her chest and looked away for a moment as if to keep herself in check. I didn't want her to be in check with me. I wanted Julia to be her unguarded self. She turned her face to look at me again, "So excuse me for trying to move on with my life. Do you think this is fun for me?" I wanted to tell her she didn't show the slightest problem in kissing him earlier but thought better of it. She sighed and paced the room for a moment.

"When's the wedding?" I finally asked.

"February." My eyebrows rose. "Don't give me that," Julia said at seeing my expression.

I waited a minute and tried to overlook the cloud that was above our heads raining on everything we once dreamt of. I shook my head. "It's my fault that this happened to you. I tried to stop it once I figured out what was happening…" I trailed off. "This is all my fault, Julia." I saw tears threatening to fall from Julia's eyes. I stepped toward her and reached to wipe them away. "I should have been there. If you had died…" Julia broke my sentence. She waved her hands. "I'm not crying about tonight," it was here that her voice broke, "I'm crying about us."

There was more she wasn't telling me. Julia walked toward the window in the hospital room and began, "She told me about the baby," Julia leaned her weight on the window sill and looked out the window, "I'd say congratulations but I know you don't want to talk about it right now. Collin," She breathed my name then turned around to face me, "When I was in this room the last time, I didn't remember what I do now. It wasn't until months later that I noticed…" Julia brought the back of her hand to her mouth and took a deep breath. She tried again, "I noticed that I was pregnant. And little by little I began to remember that I was going to tell you about the baby, our baby the night of the accident."
If there was any air left in my system it rushed out of me then. My knees shook. "Oh, Julia…"
 I hurried to her and took her in my arms. She fell apart then. Her entire body was shaking like an earthquake.
"I was making your favorite casserole and was going to tell you over dinner. But things happened…"
"The shooting," I volunteered.
"And the coma," She nodded, "And by the time I remembered any of it I ask my parents why aren't

you here with me." When I looked at her I couldn't help but be reminded of the time I rushed to the hospital when we were dating and her mother had been mistreated. I had held her then just as I held her now only things were so very different. "Then Mom tells me about you. I didn't take it well so I drive to where they told me my tombstone was, take a bat in my hands and start slamming it against the tombstone. I'm so angry and hurt that I start kicking at it," Julia grabbed hold of my shirt and clenched it with both her hands, "And the baby…" Julia's voice cracked again, "the baby died. And it's my fault. If I hadn't have gone crazy attacking my tombstone then maybe our baby would be alive." Her face was covered in tears now. I pulled her to me and let her cry on my chest. She lifted her head just as I was trying to take everything in, "It was a boy. We would have had a boy." She paused then said, "So you see, it is me who should be asking for forgiveness."

"It's not your fault, Julia. None of this is. Don't you ever blame yourself again, do you understand me?" My spirit broke. She pulled away then and tried to gather herself. As she wiped her nose on the back of her hand I said, "But I thought you couldn't have children."

"I can't." She spoke mildly. "The doctor called him a miracle. He said he'd never seen anything like it but giving the situation of me coming out of the coma, he supposed anything was possible."

I wanted to take her other hand and kiss it. So I picked up her left hand then saw her engagement ring and stopped short. How did I miss seeing it earlier? Julia watched me and as though she couldn't stand to see the look on my face, she turned her head away.

"You're not going to give blood."
"You can't tell me what to do, Collin. We're not married anymore."
"Oh yes we are. In some ways we still are." I shook my head at the stupidity of what I just said then sighed. I ran a hand through my hair. "Thank you for wanting to help and for forgiving Karen and me. I can't begin to tell you how much that means to me," It was all true, so very true. "But if you gave as much blood as we need when we need it, your body might not be able to handle it."
"I can handle it," She answered quickly. "I was raised from the dead before, remember?" Julia tried to make me smile then without saying another word, stepped out of the room and shut the door. There would be no getting rid of her.

CHAPTER TWENTY-TWO

"Alright," the nurse said as she rubbed the inside of Julia's arm with an alcohol wipe, "this will hurt a bit. We're going to leave a catheter in so we can easily access it later."
Julia nodded. The nurse looked at me funny when she saw Julia wasn't going to look away from the needle. "She's a nurse," I told her. That seemed to settle it.
Julia smiled, "Don't let him fool you. I'm only a school nurse."
The nurse stuck the needle in Julia's arm and looked back and forth between the two of us, "How long have you two been dating?"
Julia looked to me then back at the nurse. "Oh, we're not."
"But you used to?" The nurse pried with a coy grin.
We said nothing as she finished.

Julia watched me as her blood went to the bag. I couldn't help but think in a short matter of months she would be married… to someone else. And there was nothing I could do about it. The irony was cruel. But in a strange way it was a relief to be able to see Julia and not have to hide my thoughts of "I wonder how she is doing." Instead, she was here. But the reasoning was all wrong.

I stayed with Julia until the nurse finished the

first round of drawing blood. I found it difficult not to look at the bag being filled with blood. The nurse told Julia to stay put for a few hours and she would call her when she needed her again. I urged Julia to sit down in the lobby.

"I still can't believe you're doing this," I told her as she slowly walked down the hallway. I let her steady herself on my shoulder as we walked. She had just complained of feeling light headed.
"Well what else would God have me do?" I could hardly believe my ears. There were those of us that knew what the right thing to do was but then there were others like Julia that actually did it no matter the cost. I admired that about her more than I could ever say.
"Thank you," I said before I lost my nerve. She smiled up at me. "Let me get you something, you hungry?"
She shook her head, "No, I can scarcely eat after today."
"Right," I said as I rose from my seat. "Let me get you something to drink. Tea?" She laughed at me then. "Why are you laughing at me?"
"Because," she said, "you're acting awkward."
"To call this awkward would be an understatement," I said with a twinge of a smile. I left to get her some tea.

As I was gone, I couldn't help but wonder about the events in Julia's life I had missed in just a few months. Those few months seemed like a lifetime. As I made my way back to the lobby, I tried to steady myself. It was like I had suddenly transformed into the man I was when we went on our first date. She was stunning then and though shaken up tonight, she was stunning now. When I returned she was still sitting in the waiting room.

I handed Julia her cup, "*Danke*," She said as she took the cup from me. My eyebrows raised. "It's German," Julia offered. "I had some free time on my own."
"Mmm hmm." I eyed her.
"No, really. You're not the first to look at me strange. Mike and Melrose look at me funny too." Julia lifted the foam cup to her lips, blew on the brew then took a sip. Nurses were scurrying behind us in the waiting room.

    Phones were ringing and doctors were being paged. Two televisions displayed news announcers on their screens, one on each side of us. I heard all the noise but all that mattered in it, was the sound of Julia's voice and what she would say next. Four years. Four whole years boiled down to this moment and my time was running thin with her.

I don't know where I gathered the courage to ask her this, but I did, "Do you love him?"
She didn't say anything for a moment. Instead, she twirled the tea in her cup then brought it to her lips. She took a sip as if she were taking her time

but when she finally answered; I knew what her answer would be. "I'm assuming you mean Mike and not Melrose?" The end of her lip curled as she tried to lighten the mood. She looked down at her cup then up at me. "Yes," she finally said in all seriousness, "I do."

Preparing myself for her answer hadn't made it any easier to hear. My voice shook. Heck, my entire body did. "So your parents like him then?" Inside me it was like California was breaking and falling off into the ocean. I of course would have been California crumbling beneath Julia's sea of sentences.

She nodded, "They do, but Dad wasn't very thrilled when I told him he had to take down the pictures of you on the mantle to make Mike feel welcome."

"I wouldn't have either." I tried to smile at her.

"Apparently, there is still a lot to get used to." There was such truth in her words. I began to wonder what else she wanted to say to me that she couldn't bring herself to unearth.

"That's no lie," I leaned my elbows on my knees. I paused before asking, "Julia, why did you really come here?"

"I told you. I didn't want you to go through that again." It sounded so simple when she described everything that had shaken our world as that.

"Why don't you tell me why you showed up at my cabin, gave me your ring, and left with no word?"

She had me there. My words countered, "It was

your birthday."

"Right, and we're not together anymore but you just decided you would swing by and bring me a present." She placed her cup on a small table displaying outdated magazines next to her and slide her hands between her knees.

"Yes." She stared at me in disbelief. "I didn't want you to be alone on your birthday."

"I wasn't," Julia folded her arms, being careful not to touch the catheter. Of course she wasn't alone the entire night. She was with Mike then too. "You can't keep saving me, Collin."

"Why not?"

"Because we can't be in each other's lives anymore." There was something hidden behind her eyes, but I couldn't quite make it out. Was it irritation? I began to wish whatever it was included the two of us together.

I looked at her, "Because you're marrying Mike."

"And you're married to Karen."

I nodded and rose from my seat when I saw the nurse approach Julia for another blood draw. "I guess that settles it then."

"Yes," she said, "it does. Our shadows are asleep now, remember?"

I watched the nurse draw bags of blood from Julia two more times, with two extra bags to spare just in case they needed more later. Again, we said nothing as the nurse drew blood from Julia's body. I took Julia in then.

She was everything I remembered. I

wondered if Mike had touched her yet and the thought continued to torture my poor mind until the nurse finished. Jealousy rose within me. Just knowing Mike had a right to be with her in that way and I no longer did, made me squirm. Terrible thoughts played on my mind like how did they meet? Did he kiss her how she liked to be kissed? Did he know she hated wine with roses and that yellow roses were her favorite? Did he know she laughed when you kiss her ear and she never squeezed her toothpaste from the bottom of the tube? Did he know that she loved to hold hands in the car?

I steadied Julia on my shoulder again and said, "You know after the night I spent with you, I began to look at my life differently." Julia seemed taken aback. She stopped in her tracks, but I urged her to continue walking. She looked weaker now. "You were so strong spiritually. You still are. But me?" I shook my head.
"What do you mean?" she managed to ask. She looked incredibly drained. Every ounce of compassion I had went out to her. But to be honest, I was the one that needed help. She had her life together and she was living it beautifully without me.
I swallowed hard, wondering how best to describe my situation, "After you, I was terrified to put my trust in God. After all, He let this happen. He took you from me. He crushed all our dreams. He led me on. He let me believe everything was perfect

and would never fade away. And then I lost you." I inhaled quickly, all too conscious of Julia's intense gaze, "Then boom. You come back into my life like a meteorite and I can't do a thing about it. I can't stop your pain. I can't stop mine. I can't fix any of it. I was afraid to surrender my hurt and my fear over to God. I guess you could say I secretly resented him not intervening."

Julia took this in for a moment as we walked along. I helped her into her seat. She stared at the wall, toying with her fingers. I began to wonder if she had heard me at all.

Then, just as I considered getting her attention, she said, "I can see how you felt that way. I felt that way for a while too. I've asked God why things are so hard. I've asked him why he doesn't answer me, why he doesn't answer my prayers. Then," she turned to me, "I took a look at myself and saw it was me that was making things even more difficult. Who was I to question him… the creator of the universe?" Julia pushed a piece of hair behind her ear almost as if she were embarrassed, "Oh sure, I knew God loved me but it didn't seem to have quite the effect it once had. He seemed so distant to me. I guess you could say that was my fork in the road moment." She looked down and continued, "Mom told me that God wanted to heal me. God wanted to put the pieces of my life back together again and make me whole but he wasn't going to force me to hand over the pieces to him if

I didn't want to. By holding on to my pain I wasn't letting God take care of me."
I smiled at her in awe. "I can't say I am where I would like to be but I am making progress." I hoped that one day I would be able to accept things the way it appeared she had.
Julia smiled back, "I believe in you, Collin. I always have. But I believe in God more and I know he can and will help you if you will let him. We have to open the door and let him in." She was a wise woman.

I told Julia that I quit my job at the law firm and was now working at the lumber yard again. When needed, I represented them in court and gave legal advice as far as environmental issues were concerned. She was stunned and praised my decision. I told her she'd encouraged me to do it. In response, she simply shrugged.

A wave of silence passed and suddenly I couldn't stand it any longer. "Does it get easier?"
"What?" Julia asked as she looked to me.
I felt like I was tripping over the words. "...Living without someone you care about? How do you forget them? Does the pain stay?"
I searched her eyes for a moment.
Julia appeared shaken. Embarrassed, she tucked a strand of hair behind her ear and looked away. She thought for a moment then said, "I wouldn't say it gets easier. You just... get used to it... to the pain. You learn to live with it. Some days it's

bearable and others…" her voice trailed then she brought it back again. She looked into my eyes, "You never forget. You do what you are required to but you never forget."
I couldn't bring myself to speak. Nothing else was said.

Three more hours later, the doctor came to us and told me that Karen was looking a little better. He said he thought she had a better chance at making it now and wouldn't need Julia to give any more blood, but if by chance they did, they would call her. The news had a double effect on me. I was glad they didn't require Julia's blood anymore and at least some once of me was thankful Karen was out of the grip of death, but I didn't want to see Julia go. With her departure I knew I was stuck with Karen who I couldn't stand to be near much less spend the rest of my life with. Julia and I said nothing in response as the doctor gave us the news.

I took her by the arm and placed it on mine to steady her. I walked Julia out of the hospital and to her car. She said nothing the entire time and neither did I. If I didn't know any better I would think she was shaking. We stepped out of the hospital's ground floor and onto the parking lot. I could almost hear the ticking of the seconds growing louder with every step we took.

"I guess this is it then," I said more out of obligation than anything else.

She nodded and whispered softly, "I guess so."
Julia read my eyes for what felt like minutes then pulled a chain out of her shirt and showed it to me. My wedding band was hanging from it. Knowing she'd been carrying it around jolted me.
"I guess you won't be needing this back?"
"No," I shook my head, stunned. "Are you going to be okay?"
"Me?" She smiled, "I'll be super." She knew I wouldn't buy that. I shoved my hands in my pockets and pretended I did. I was concerned about her marrying Mike. I was concerned about the whole scene but reminded myself to put the matter in God's hands.

My heart quickened. The words good bye were eminent and looming over us like a cloud.

"Take care of yourself, Julia."
"I will." She unlocked her car. I opened the door for her then watched her climb inside. She thrust her key in the ignition and but hesitated before cranking the engine.
I seized the moment and leaned over the driver's door. "Julia?"
"Yeah?" She was breathing hard now.
"I'm never going to see you again, am I?" A lump was edging in my throat.
"No, probably not." Her voice was breathy.
I waited several seconds. Julia was still facing straight ahead with a panic stricken look on her face. "Something the matter?" Maybe there was

more she had to say to me.
She nodded. "You?"
"Yes," I answered her.
"Why is this so hard?" Julia turned to look at me then. Her eyes pierced mine.
"I don't know. But if it makes you feel any better, you did the right thing."
"So did you," She said. I smiled at her. I'd miss seeing that beautiful face of hers. It used to be so easy and simple being around each other but now the forces against us were too strong and complicated. The right thing to do was stay away from each other.
"Thank you for telling me... about our baby. It wasn't easy for you to tell me but you have no idea how grateful I am that you did," I paused a moment to recapture my wits about me. "Things could have been so different for us. I know you wanted to have a baby, our baby, and so did I. I'm so sorry you went through that on your own. I feel awful that I wasn't there for you to help you. Instead, I only caused you more pain. Please, forgive me, Julia."
"You didn't know. There is nothing to forgive." Julia reached out her hand for mine and I squeezed it. Her mercy, forgiveness and compassion touched me. There was so much of God's spirit dwelling in her.
"What--" I began then stopped myself, "what would you have named him if he had lived... our son?"
Julia closed her eyes, trying not to cry then said,

"Adam." It was my middle name.
"Adam. I like it," I said as she opened her eye. We stared at each other for quite a while. Julia bounced her knees and fiddled with the keys on her key ring. She was so nervous. I had to end it or it would never end.
"I wish you nothing but the absolute best." She nodded and strapped her seat belt on. "And Julia?"

I wanted to tell her I would miss her and how much I wished things could still work out for us. That maybe someday we would have a chance to be all that we felt we were meant to be. I wanted to tell her I missed her and would always miss her and that a part of me loves her and will always love her. But once again, it was wrong to do so. So instead, I said nothing.

But to my surprise she said, "I know, Collin. I do too."

She forced herself to drive off then and I forced myself to stay planted where I was and not run after her.

CHAPTER TWENTY-THREE

JULIA

How do I begin to describe the emptiness I felt as I drove away? I had convinced myself we were doing the right thing. I'd done everything God would have me to do and yet here we were stuck in this mess with no way out. God would have wanted me to let Collin live his new life with Karen and that is exactly what I did even though it ripped my heart out to do so. Apparently my daily sacrifices did not matter to God. It seemed like such an iniquity. I shook my head and ran my left hand through my hair. I could never escape it, escape him.

The memories of Collin were inimical and they relentlessly followed me everywhere. At night the reality of the situation would weigh so heavily on my chest that I could not sleep. Normally I fixed a pot of tea and paced the kitchen as I waited for it to boil. Nights were the absolute worse. During the day time I could at least keep myself busy pretending not to miss him but at night there was no task that could hide the emptiness that I possessed without him. I wanted to throw things. I wanted to scream my bloody head off and not have to explain myself to anyone. I wanted to cry and not have to hide the tears. I wanted to break down and lay curled up in my crumpled sheets, cling to the pillow on my bed and pretend it was him hugging back.

had just thought it was difficult to carry on without Collin before but now, now that I'd seen him and held him it was exponentially difficult. Now that I'd said goodbye what seemed like a billion times it was never enough. It was never goodbye with us, probably because we didn't want it to be. I'd thrown out every memory of our life together years ago except the little picture of us in the frame on my night stand. Once I realized throwing our possessions in the trash did not help at all, I placed our picture on the stand. Maybe if I came to terms with my new reality and faced it I would not be affected anymore. But I was. No matter what I did or didn't do I was haunted.

It was as though nothing could satisfy me. My soul was chapped and the constant cravings I felt to see him again refused to ease. I couldn't understand why or how long we were supposed to suffer for my mistake. I could not believe God to be that cruel and yet the nightmare continued to engulf me.

Collin was out there…. Alive…. Without me. Something in me died the night I drove away from the hospital. It wasn't right that we loved each other and were not allowed to be together. It wasn't right that we finally found each other again only to be ripped apart. It was a sick joke that we loved each other and would now be forced to spend the rest of our lives without one another.

No one at work seemed to notice anything was wrong. They didn't ask, I didn't tell. Besides, it's not like I could say, "What's wrong? I'm in love with another woman's husband. That's what's wrong." But soon enough the papers caught up on the whole story. By papers I mean the two newspapers based in the county. They read: "Dead Woman Comes to Life, Wife Shot", "Modern Day Lazarus", "Raised from the Dead", "Husband of Two Wives and the One He Came Rushing to Save." I could go on and on mentioning the columns written about us. You'd think living in a small town in the southern swamps of Louisiana, privacy would be a priority but not where the newspapers were concerned. I was portrayed as the villain who stole Karen's husband away from her. Karen was portrayed as the injured person who went postal because of the hell we put her through. Collin was painted as the hopeless lover running to rescue me and caught in a tangled web. It was rumored that Collin had to have known I was alive all these years. Some people thought he was a modern day pimp balancing Karen and I at the same time. I was looked down on for not contacting him to tell him the truth. Karen though pitied by some, was seen as the certifiable nut in the drama and I couldn't say I agreed more to that statement.

    I believed there was some truth to be had from the columns. Yes, Karen went Rambo when she tried to kill me. Yes, she was trying to hurt Collin by doing so. Yes, we had made her already existing insecurities worse. But I don't want to apologize for loving him. We were right in loving each other before. It wasn't our fault that we still loved each other. He tried so very hard and I am still trying to fight it but our love is strong, stronger now I believe than it ever has been.

But I had to move on. And so did he. The question was how.

Mike, I knew, sensed something was wrong. I'd showed him the papers and explained, as briefly as possible what happened. Somehow what happened between Collin and I didn't seem like anyone else's business. Mike was so good about it. He'd shake his head and said how sorry he was that I had to go through this. He'd offered to spend the night at my cabin the night of the incident so I would feel safe and he could make sure no one else would try to hurt me. He drove me to the police station. But how could I tell him that I merely wanted to be left alone? Mike held my hand through the entirety of the questioning. When it was over, he dropped me off and tried once again to convince me not to stay at the cabin alone. I assured him I would be alright and went inside to feed Melrose.

I found him meowing on my bed. He began purring when he saw me. I kicked my shoes off in the doorway and dropped my keys and purse on the floor. I picked him up and kissed the back of his head, like I did when I first got him. He purred even louder then. I placed him back on the bed and refilled his food bowl. When I returned to the bedroom, Melrose didn't budge. Normally he would run for the food as he heard it clink in his bowl but tonight he seemed to sense that I needed him. I fained a weak smile and curled up on my bed. I took Melrose and laid him in my arms. He wasn't the most affectionate cat but he didn't protest my hugging him. I sighed and sat on the edge of the bed. It was the side Collin slept on when he was here. I stared at the wall. I was sitting at home with my cat when Collin was in the hospital with his wife dying. I had my cat. He had no one. I threw my head back and heaved another deep sigh. There was my answer. I couldn't let Collin go through losing someone else he loved. So, I went.

CHAPTER TWENTY-FOUR

JULIA

If I hadn't helped Karen, the odds are she would have died. I knew that. Still, I felt responsible and I wanted to help. That's exactly what I told Mike. I would have preferred not to tell Mike. And I especially would have preferred it if my parents would have stopped calling me every hour to see if I was alright. Of course I wasn't alright.
There wasn't a day that went by that I didn't ache to see Collin again or an hour that passed that I did not wonder where he was or how he was doing or if he ever thought of me.

I spent most of my time on the cabin's porch overlooking the bayou. I could hear the sounds of crickets humming and pelicans crowing. There I could get lost in the sounds of nature and not in the images that flooded my head of Collin. Images I would have been much better off without. Sometimes I would run along the bayou or if I felt like a change, I'd jog along the lonely dirt road leading to my cabin. There I felt safe from the stares I was sure to get jogging in town. I loved the sounds out there and the creepy look of the swamp trees, some of them centuries old. I liked to imagine the French fur trappers coming to Louisiana in their boats along the swampland and their wives waiting for them back home. I thought of the many families who had made this swamp part of their life before me and the certainty that there would be countless families enjoying it after me. Time would go on with or without me. Thinking back, it was then that I decided to continue the wedding plans.

When the sun faded behind the orange bayou water, Mike would arrive to bring me dinner. He knew I wanted to avoid the small crowd at any restaurant. He was good to me like that. He was a solid, strong, inspirational man and I felt blessed to know him. Even so, his presence meant Collin was no longer in my life. And he was not Collin. I began to resent that. I began to resent a lot of things.

Some nights I unplugged the telephone line just so I could sit and hear the beating of my own heart. I had to make sure I was still alive. I was so tired of being tired. I was exhausted from living my life without him. And then I would remind myself once again of why things had to be the way they were.

I worked my way toward the kitchen and retrieved a bottle of red wine from the cupboard and poured myself half a small glass. I'd never been much on alcohol yet there I was swirling the wine in a glass under my nose. I inhaled its aroma much like Collin and I had learned during our honeymoon on one of the days we were snowed in on the resort. I laughed as I thought of Collin's face gawking at the process of producing wine and its many flavors. I too had been utterly clueless about the wine industry though even now I could not claim expertise.

I took a sip of the wine and swished it around on the top of my tongue. It was pungent, strong and strangely bittersweet at the same time. I swallowed it and felt it burn slowly as it went down. I placed the glass on my small dining room table I'd managed to wedge into the kitchen. I toyed with the glass for a moment and contemplated my current coping methods. My head dropped in my hand then I shook my head. This was wrong. It was all wrong.

I gently rose from my chair and dumped the remaining wine in the glass in the kitchen sink then retreated to the bedroom where I answered Mike's goodnight phone call and turned off the lights. I took Melrose in my arms and held him close to my chest. Tears began to fall onto Melrose's thick white fur. He meowed so I pet the top of his head and apologized as though he could understand. I flopped my head onto the cool pillow and prayed to fall asleep.

CHAPTER TWENTY-FIVE

COLLIN

Karen lived for nearly two weeks after she came home from the hospital. One night as I slept, I heard her gasping for air. I rose from the bed and went over to her. I still can't be sure what she was trying to say as she grasped her chest, but I think she said "Sorry."

The court was waiting for her to get better before they tried her. In the time she was at home, she seemed more reserved. She rarely talked anymore. It was almost as if she felt remorse for what she had done. She didn't sleep in our bed anymore. Instead, she slept in the hospital bed near mine. I was supposed to bathe her but when she first came home I couldn't bring myself to do it so I had her mother bathe her.

I was standing over Karen as she passed away. I called 911. The emergency technicians pronounced her as dead then rushed her body into the ambulance. They brought her to the ER where Karen's doctor could hopefully deliver the baby. And they did. He came out covered in blood with a strong set of lungs. He was premature but as healthy as could be.

A week later I brought him home to the room Karen had set up for him. She had painted the walls blue and hung a sailboat mobile above his crib. I had arranged stuffed animals in his crib and on his toy box. I'd even helped Karen paint his room and hung red curtains. It was so odd having him finally there. I couldn't help but feel remorse for Karen not being able to share in the birth of our baby. He rarely slept for the first few months and I couldn't say I blamed him for it. He just lost his mother. Every child knows when they lose someone vital whether they have been in the world for twelve years or twelve seconds. It was just the two of us.

My brother Alvin finally told me how Karen knew where to find Julia. He had told her where we were. I can't say I took it as well as I wish I would have. I avoided him for a week. Eventually forgiveness won out. He and his wife would baby sit whenever I had to work late at the lumber yard.

Once the baby began crawling, Eddy would bark wherever he went. When the baby took his first steps, Eddy was right behind him and I was ready with the video camera.

I tried my best to make sure he knew who his mother was and what sort of woman Karen was before the end of her life. He deserved to know about his mother, but I will never tell him about what she did. I just told him Karen loved him very much and couldn't wait to hold her baby boy.

On Thursdays Dad would stop by and pretend to make himself useful. More often than not, he sat in the recliner and stared at my son like he was an alien. It was then I knew that mom had done all the 2 am feedings. It was she who had bathed us, fed us and cared for us. This man seemed like a stranger to children. I, of course, had no idea what I was doing. In my defense, I can honestly say Karen had been the one to read all the baby manuals. I soon found myself pouring over them as well. At night when the house was finally quiet somewhere between midnight and two a.m., my thoughts would drift to Julia.

It was February now. Since the attempted murder fiasco, the newspaper and television stations had picked up on Julia's story. Now everyone knew she was alive. Everyone also knew the exact date she would marry Mike Stephens. I'd actually discovered his last name from the paper as well. The nearer the days drew to Julia's wedding day, the more I frequented the church. I talked to the pastor for the first time since Julia's supposed death. I placed lilies and a picture of our son on Karen's grave. I had Alvin and his wife keep the baby so I could paddle the bayou where I found no one lived in Julia's cabin anymore. I jogged with Eddy in the mornings before work. I did anything to avoid showing up at Julia's wedding as an uninvited guest. I did anything to remind myself why I wasn't the groom standing next to her. Yet somehow I managed to arrive at her wedding on the 13th.

I stood outside the stone fence and peeked out from behind a corner, toward the rod iron gate.

They were marrying in Iris Park near the water fountain. I'd always imagined Julia marrying inside a church like we had. I forced myself to keep my feet planted where they were and not run around looking for her. I wanted to ask her to choose me. I wanted to remind her of the way we were and the way we still could be. I dreamt of taking her in my arms and shouting how much I still loved her. But then I thought of home. I couldn't ask her to forget everything that had happened. I couldn't ask her to come home to a baby that wasn't hers and a house full of Karen. I loved her more than that. She was worth so much more than that.

Frank and Alice were seated in the front row. I recognized the back of their heads immediately. As I saw Julia enter the garden from behind a gazebo, I was flooded with memories of our wedding. Julia was gorgeous and she looked… happy. Who was I to take that from her? She had waited too long to be happy and now that she was, I wouldn't dare be the one to steal it from her. I pressed my nose to the iron rod fence and fought to stay where I was. It was the right thing to do. I prayed hard and surrendered my life again to the Lord. I watched Julia long enough to see her stand beside Mike and take his hand then I couldn't watch anymore. Mike was a blessed man. I only hoped he knew how blessed.
I inhaled a sharp breath and forced myself to walk away. I was showing my love for Julia the best way I knew how. And maybe now she could

know the love I would never be able to show her.

CHAPTER TWENTY-SIX

Years passed. My son was old enough to go to pre-school for the first time. I was a body full of nerves. I'd watched him teethe, grow, crawl, wobble, and walk. And now he was walking his way into pre-school, granted I was still holding his hand. I dropped him off outside his classroom door and gave him the biggest hug I have probably ever given anyone in my life. He had Karen's nose but everything else about him looked like me when I was three. He was mischievous to the point that I felt I had to watch him closely, especially with driving my car. I learned my lesson when I left him alone in the back seat while I went to grab the mail one Saturday. When I turned my back, he had somehow managed to weasel his way out of his child seat and crawled into the driver's side. When I ran full fledge to the driver's door and opened it, he was reaching for the stick shift and hitting it. I've been paranoid about having him in my car ever since. I knew he would give his teacher mischief. When I looked at him, I still saw my newborn son lying in my arms.

I got better at calming my nerves when I dropped him off at pre-school. The greater miracle was that I was learning to trust God with my son instead of just trusting God with the rest of my life. Then I got a call from his pre-school teacher saying he was sick and I'd better come pick him up. Talk about protective parent mode. I was out of the lumber yard in no time and raced to the pre-school steps.

Children were in classes. I could hear a class repeating the alphabet after their teacher as she pointed to the letters on the chalkboard. I smiled, thinking my son had probably been the one to lead the class in reciting the alphabet. He was so smart. I'd introduced him to the alphabet when he was only a year old. He picked it up quick. But now as I continued walking down the long hallway toward the nurse's office I didn't know if I'd find him with chicken pox or throw up on the floor. I pushed the door open on the left which read "Nurse." I'd never been in there before and to be honest, my memories of going to a school nurse in pre-school were never fond. Then the bright thought occurred to me that perhaps my son had gotten into mischief and hurt himself in the process.

I pushed open the door and saw him sitting on the edge of what looked like a mini booth.

He jumped from his seat slower than normal and ran for me shouting "Dad!" I engulfed him in a hug.
"What's the matter, Adam? Are you okay? "I stroked his dark hair. He appeared okay except for his eyes which were a little puffy. It looked like he had been crying. I pulled him to me again and kissed him on the cheek. "Where does it hurt?" He

pointed to his throat. Hoping for a solid answer, I looked up at the nurse. She had her back to me, rummaging through files. "Excuse me miss, what's wrong with him?"

The nurse turned slowly and it was then I saw her. Her hair was shorter, nearly chin length but her eyes still sparkled.
It was Julia.
She took in a sharp breath when she saw me and nearly dropped the files she was holding in her hands. For a moment we said nothing. I merely looked at her like I was seeing a ghost. I swallowed hard and tried to calm the butterflies raging in the pit of my stomach. I rose from squatting to hug Adam and patted him on the head.

He turned around and faced her then said, "Daddy, Miss Julia made me feel better." Adam tugged on my arm as he said it.
"Hi, Collin," She said and smiled. Julia placed her hands on the desk in front of her and dropped her files there.
"Julia," I nearly stumbled over her name. It seemed to amuse her.
Julia looked down and began to busy herself with the papers on her desk. "He complained to the teacher that his throat was hurting. He's been crying and coughing so I checked for a fever and sure enough, he had one. I gave him some cough syrup and a Tylenol to break the fever but you'll

want to take him home and put him to bed. I've seen this sort of thing a lot lately. It'll take about two or three days for him to be well enough to return to school."

I just stared at her. It was like I was a stranger to her now. I was merely the parent of a sick child and she was merely the nurse informing me of his health. I blinked at her, waiting for her to say something personal. But she didn't. I chewed on my lip for about four seconds then searched for something to say.

"How are you?"
Julia lifted her head then. Her eyes were soft. "I'm good, thanks for asking."
"And Mike?"
Julia hesitated for a second then replied with, "I wouldn't know. I imagine he is fine."
I furrowed my brow. "What do you mean you don't know? I saw you at the wedding. What happened to him?"
A look of shock registered on her face, "You saw me at my wedding?"
"…Yes" I answered slowly.
She shook her head. "I didn't go through with it."
I couldn't believe my ears. But she had told me she loved him. "Why?" I asked. It seemed like the only semi appropriate question I could manage.
Julia stepped out from behind the desk and grabbed some cough syrup off her desk and handed it to Adam. She bent down to him and

stroked his cheek. "You be a good boy for your daddy and make sure he gives this to you twice a day." Adam nodded. Julia winked at me as she rose. She was ignoring my question.
"Julia?"
"It doesn't matter anymore," She answered quickly. Julia walked over to her desk again and rummaged in a drawer for a pen. She began writing on a pad of paper with it.
"Daddy, you know Miss Julia?" Adam asked innocently.
I wanted to slap myself, "Yes, Adam. Daddy knows Miss Julia."
"How come I never met Miss Julia before Daddy?" Adam prodded. Children and questions. I always thought his questions were cute until now.
Julia tore off a piece of paper from the pad she was writing on and handed it to me, "You need to give this to the attendance clerk when you leave. She'll have you sign a paper saying you picked him up." She turned away from me and sat at her desk. She opened a file and began to make notes in it with her pen. "Adam. That's a good strong name," I heard her say.
I met her eyes. "I thought so. I once had a wonderful woman tell me about it." Julia avoided my gaze then a few seconds later, took a deep breath then said, "I hope Karen is better. I hope you're doing good too. Take care of Adam, Collin. He looks just like you and acts like it too."

I turned to go and picked up little Adam. I

carried him on my hip as I exited the door. I
thought I could feel Julia's eyes watching me as
we exited. I peered around for the attendance
clerk and handed her the slip. I asked her to watch
little Adam for me. She gave me the strangest look
then agreed the same as if I had ruined her entire
day.

"Daddy will be right back," I told Adam as I
hurried for the nurse's door again.

When I swung the door open the second time
around, Julia popped up from her seat.

She was astounded, "Collin, this place is for sick
children. You're not a child and you're not sick so
I must ask you to leave."
I ignored her request and walked right up to her.
She was breathing heavy. I took a deep breath,
desperate for her to know the truth now that I
could finally say it, and altogether desperate to
know why she didn't marry Mike. "Karen is much
better, thank you for asking." Julia looked at me
like I had lost my mind. "She's dead."
Julia shook her head. "That's impossible. I was
there when the doctor said she was out of danger.
She was out of danger, wasn't she?" I nodded.
"Was it my blood?" Julia looked terrified that
perhaps she had somehow played a part in
Karen's death.
"No, Julia, it wasn't you," I paused recalling the
event as it took place. "Her chest filled up with

blood again and there was nothing they could do. She didn't want to lose the baby so there were no options."

Julia continued to shake her head as she leaned on the edge of her desk. She brought a hand to her mouth and squinted her eyes, trying to make sense of it all. "I'm sorry, Collin," she finally said.

"Why didn't you marry Mike?" the words flew out of my mouth.

Julia licked her lips and considered how best to answer me. "He wasn't you."

My heart beat wildly in my chest. "But you loved him."

"I know," She was afraid to meet my eyes, "but he still wasn't you. Tell me something, Collin. If Karen died shortly after she was in the hospital, then why didn't you stop me from going to marry Mike?" Julia gathered her composure.

The answer was flying around in my head. She still had the ability to catch me off guard. That was the last question I expected her to ask. "I couldn't ask you to come home to a house full of Karen and her baby. And besides, you loved Mike. I thought you didn't love me anymore. I wanted you to be happy."

"Adam is your child too," I couldn't help but smile as she said that. "Of course I still loved you, Collin," she said with an incredulous look, "Didn't you still love me?"

"Yes," I answered without a moment's hesitation. My hand shook as I reached for hers. "I still love you, Julia. I've never stopped loving you."

Her eyes sparkled. I went to touch her cheek but she turned her back to me. I tried to see what was wrong then she said, "You don't know how long I've waited to hear you say that." Julia's body shook and tears began to fall.
I wrapped her in my arms and held her as tight as I could, "You don't know how long I've waited to say it."

I turned her toward me and Julia leaned her head on my shoulder. I wiped stay tears from her face then lifted her chin with my index finger. Julia's lips formed a sweet smile at feeling my touch on her face. She closed her eyes. I leaned in feeling like a little boy, sweaty and nervous at being near the only girl I'd ever really loved and brought my lips to hers. It was better than I remembered it to be. I don't recall how long we'd been kissing when I heard a little giggle come from the doorway. Adam popped his head in and Julia and I jumped.

"I think she's pretty too, Daddy," He said with a little smile.

EPILOGUE

It wasn't but a week later that Julia and I remarried. Little Adam and I moved out of our place and into Julia's small home near the bayou. It wasn't the cabin, but it was still nice and cozy. Adam took to it and Julia immediately. Eddy on the other hand, made a game of chasing Melrose all over the house. Frank and Alice visited often. They treated Adam like he was their own grandson. And Julia always showed him a heart full of love. She sang him lullabies before he went to bed at night. She played games with him, but his favorite to play with her was hide and go seek. I just made sure he couldn't hide in the car. It took Julia a while to realize he had driving skills at the age of three but after we chased him down the driveway, she figured it out.

Adam started to call Julia mommy. I remember the first time he did it. He was playing outside with Eddy and ran without watching where he was going. I was changing the oil in my car when I heard him fall. He skinned his knee on the concrete in the driveway. I ran for him and scooped him into my arms. But he didn't want me. He wanted Julia. He began crying, snot pouring from his nose. "Mommy!" His little lungs expanded. He kept screaming mommy until I brought him inside to Julia. He ran up to her and wrapped his little arms around her leg.

Julia looked up at me, her eyes as wide as

saucers. I shrugged at her. Julia bent down just in time for Adam to stretch his arms out to her and throw them around her neck. "Mommy!" he cried. Julia smiled and blinked a lot, probably to keep from crying. She picked him up and covered his contorted face in kisses. She grabbed a tissue and wiped tears from his face. "Kiss" he said, as he pointed to his knee. Julia cleaned the wound with alcohol then kissed it. Adam laughed. After she placed antibiotic ointment and a Band-Aid on his wounded knee, she picked him up in her arms and carried him around for a little while, smiling. He ended up falling asleep. She tucked him in his bed for a nap then he said, "I love you, Mommy." Julia came out of his bedroom crying. I just smiled at her and wrapped her in a hug. "I think he loves you," I told her.

"I love him too," she said. I don't think my heart as ever been so filled with love as it was in that moment.

It was about four years later that Julia cooked me my favorite casserole. She had candles lit on the table and was singing a tune I couldn't quite make out in the kitchen as she gathered plates. I brought the sweet tea to the table and poured some in both our glasses. Adam was spending the night at Frank and Alice's so we had the house to ourselves. Julia was beaming like a child at Christmas. I laughed at her expression.

"Collin," she grabbed my hand and squeezed it, "I have something to tell you." It was then that I

remembered the last time she had made me a casserole with sweet tea and planned on lighting candles on the dinner table. Julia bit her lip then said, "We're pregnant."
I blinked.
"Honey, did you hear what I said?"

I nodded and picked her up out of her seat. I spun her around the dining room. A slipper flew off Julia's feet but she didn't seem to care. We both laughed. That was the night I found out God had given us a second child, our very own Emma.

I just thought my heart was as full as it could get but God kept expanding it. He gave me my Julia back. He gave me Adam and now little Emma. Life was better than I imagined it to be. I wouldn't be running anywhere.

ABOUT THE AUTHOR

Danielle lives under the big Texas sky with her two Golden Retrievers. She is a dance teacher and exercise instructor. Danielle is fluent in both English and French. She can be found trying her hand at photography. At twenty-six years old Danielle is the seasoned author of fourteen novels.

She wrote her first novel, "Against All Odds: The Ruby Princess" at fourteen years old. She later published it at seventeen. Danielle became a professional model in print and on runway at ten years old and a professional actress at twelve; doing commercials and acting in a pilot series with Haley Duff and Shelly Duvall. She's won many international pageants and has been performing from an early age, winning awards for her choreography and dancing.

Danielle began writing songs at the age of six and writing short stories at ten years old. She is a graduate of Lamar University with Bachelor degrees in Political Science and French with a minor in Writing and Teacher's Certification. She is also a seasoned missionary. She loves playing guitar to her own beat, dancing in grocery store aisles, and singing whenever the urge strikes. Danielle often travels with pen in hand.

CONNECT WITH DANIELLE ONLINE

Official Author Website:
www.DanielleBienvenu.com

Smashwords:
www.smashwords.com/profile/view/DanielleBienvenu

Facebook:
www.facebook.com/DanielleNicole.author

Facebook Fan Page:
www.facebook.com/DanielleBienvenu.author

Twitter:
www.twitter.com/DBienvenu

Myspace:
http://www.myspace.com/daniellebienvenu

Her work can also be found online at:

Amazon
Barnes & Noble
Books A Million
Google
iBooks

Printed in Great Britain
by Amazon.co.uk, Ltd.,
Marston Gate.